M000077985

The COWBOY Next Door

Cowboy Hero, Book 1

BARBARA McMAHON

The Cowboy Next Door
Copyright © 2011, 2021 Barbara McMahon
All Rights Reserved

No part of this book may be used or reproduced in any manner whatsoever without written permission from the author except in the case of brief quotations embodied in critical articles or reviews.

This is a work of fiction. Names, characters, places and incidents are products of the author's imagination and are used fictitiously. Any resemblance to actual events, locales, organizations or persons living or dead is entirely coincidental.

The
COWBOY
Next Door

One

Amanda Smith alighted from the bus, shocked as the heat of the day engulfed her. She'd been traveling in comfort for hours, even verging on being too cool, as the bus had sped its way eastward from the coast. Aware of the brightness of the cloudless day through the tinted windows, but not the heat, she'd given no thought to the temperature until she plunged into it.

The hot noonday sun shone down with searing rays, the lack of breeze ensuring that the heat hung close to the earth. A far cry from the Pacific coast she'd left earlier this morning.

Looking around, however, she smiled, almost giddy with delight to finally be here.

Twice before she'd passed through Timber, California. Now she was here for a long visit--actually to look into the possibilities of settling here on a semi-permanent basis. As much as her career would permit.

The small main street shimmered beneath the relentless sun, heat waves distorting the shop fronts and reflecting non-existent puddles on the asphalt road. Slowly she walked along the side of the bus, awaiting the driver who'd unload her suitcases. Unload hers alone, it appeared, as no one else had disembarked. Once done, he'd drive on.

The depot for Timber consisted of a small wooden attachment to the gas station: one window for tickets and a wooden bench serving as the waiting area. What did a person do in the rain? she wondered idly as she waited for her luggage.

"I'll have your things in a jiffy, miss."

The bus driver joined her on the hot pavement. With a quick jerk, he opened the side panel, revealing the capacious luggage compartment. Reaching among the bags, he unerringly pulled out her large, soft-sided suitcase and the battered guitar case.

"These are all, right, miss?"

"Yes, thanks." Amanda took them from him. Hoisting her guitar case on her shoulder by the strap, she pulled up the handle to the suitcase.

Slamming down the compartment door, he sketched a small salute and returned to the bus.

Amanda turned and approached the ticket window. She'd passed through this small mountain town before, across the narrow bridge on the approach to Timber—a concrete structure spanning the Mokelumne River, connecting Timber with the western part of the state. This time, though, she wasn't passing through.

She was staying for a while.

Her dark hair absorbing the heat, Amanda felt the full strength of the sun beating through to her scalp. Perspiration beaded on her forehead, ran between her breasts. She took a deep breath. It didn't help; the air was hot, still.

She rolled her suitcase closer to the wooden building and turned to watch the bus as it lumbered down the street and began its climb as the highway wound upwards, heading north, to greater heights.

For a town named Timber, the most notable aspect of the trees was the lack of them. True, at the city limits, the Sierra forest began, but within sight there were few trees, none of great size or age.

Her eyes followed the bus until it rounded the bend and was lost from view. She then looked around.

The town was small. This she knew. But the actual sight of it from the ground only emphasized it was a far cry from LA. From the furthermost building to the bus depot where she stood didn't cover two city blocks in length, if that. She could see the entire town from her vantage point.

Of course, that's what she was seeking. A small community, as different from the cities she had been working in as she could find.

This place was perfect. Few cars, no garish neon signs and only a couple of buildings taller than a single story. Smiling involuntarily, Amanda felt a warm delight flow through her, a strong feeling of nostalgia, of deja vu, and of homecoming.

The fronts to the various stores and shops were irregular and without pattern. Two were two- storied, others single stories. Still others were faced with a high facade masking their small status.

Red was a popular color; she counted five stores painted red. White was also popular, with beige, blue and yellow also in evidence. There was even a brick building to her left, an unusual sight in the Sierra Nevada.

"Can I help you?"

She turned to find a small, wizened man at the ticket window gravely studying her.

"Is there somewhere I can leave my luggage for a while?" she asked, indicating the pieces.

"Sure, put them on the bench. I'll keep an eye on them for you. They'll be okay there."

Frowning with hesitation, she looked at the bench. It was out of direct view from his window.

Then she glanced down the sleepy street. The few people in sight on the pavements either chatted easily with one another or called out friendly greetings as others passed. No one was interested in her or her luggage.

She turned back.

"Thank you, I won't be too long."

Rolling the suitcase against the building, she rested the guitar case against it. With a smile, she turned back to the ticket agent.

"I'll watch "em, miss, don't you fret." He looked like somebody's grandfather.

She nodded, hitching her shoulder bag up higher. Again she surveyed the town, this time seeking a specific place, slowly moving to an establishment which caught her eye.

Gold Country Homes and Ranches, the sign hanging over the sidewalk in front of the large plate glass window proclaimed. The lettering was faded, weathered, hanging from rusty chains, stationary in the hot sun. A dozen or so photos were taped to the window, each a picture of a house

THE COWBOY NEXT DOOR

or an expanse of land, all presumably for sale.

She pushed on the glass door feeling the blessed coolness as soon as she stepped inside.

There were only two people in the office--a gray-haired man seated behind a desk in the rear of the large room and an equally gray-haired woman seated opposite him. While there were three other desks in the office, with evidence of occupation, phones, maps, open survey books, their owners were absent. Perhaps showing property.

Amanda wasn't sure the couple in the rear had heard her enter and she waited patiently for them to finish. The older woman was speaking. She had a loud, whiny voice.

"... but not to Mac. I'm absolutely adamant about that, Martin. Not to Mac!"

"Be reasonable, Cora."

The man seemed patient, as one who'd been over this before.

"No one else will take it. If you're leaving, why do you care who gets it? Take what money you can get and go on along to Phoenix. Julie'll be so glad to have you close. Forget us here."

"No, Martin, not to Mac." She was firm. "How do you know no one else will take it? Advertise and find out."

"Cora, if I advertise, I have to sell it to whoever offers the best price. It's the law. I cannot refuse to accept an offer just because it comes from someone you don't like."

"Then don't advertise," she muttered.

"Then nobody'll know it's available and you'll never get it sold."

He leaned back in his chair.

"It's not worth much anyway. The house is small, old, away from town, with no near neighbors and few amenities, surrounded by trees and precious little else. You'll be hard pressed to find anyone who wants a place like that Cora, be realistic."

"I might be interested," Amanda spoke up.

The woman swiveled to see who'd spoken.

The man leaned sideways in his chair to see around Cora.

Amanda knew they'd see a tall, thin woman dressed in jeans and a cotton shirt. Her dark hair was drawn back in a single plait down her back. Large tinted glasses hid her expression like a mask.

"Who are you?" the woman named Cora asked.

"My name is Mandy Smith."

She walked to the back.

"Not from around here, are you, miss?" the man asked, his tone more cordial than Cora's.

She could be, her faded jeans, scuffed boots and cotton shirt was the same attire everyone wore nowadays. Everybody young, that is.

"No, but I'm interested in settling here. I came in to find a place."

He looked at her for a moment, rubbing his chin, obviously phrasing his words carefully. "The, uh, place in question is for sale not for rent."

"Yes, so I gathered from your conversation. I'd like to see it. I might be interested ."

"It's out of town a few miles," he said.

"With no near neighbors and lots of trees," she repeated.

"Yes, that's right, girl," the old woman said. "It's a mite run down, needs a little work, but it's real pleasant to sit out on the deck and hear the breeze rustle through the trees in the evenings."

She turned back to the man. "Take her up, Martin. Let her see what it's like."

"There's nobody here, Cora, to answer the phone. I can't just leave until one of the other agents returns."

"I'll answer if they ring. Just till Dottie comes back. Go on, Martin. Miss Smith might want it. If so that would solve everything."

"It's for sale," Martin said again, as if explaining an important fact to a child.

"Don't let my clothes mislead you," Amanda said gently. "If I like it, I can afford it."

"Go on, Martin," Cora urged.

"Okay, okay."

He rose, picked up his hat from the nearby rack and came around his desk.

"Okay, young lady, we'll go see it. Watch the phones, Cora."

Amanda preceded him from the office, pausing on the pavement.

"I don't have a car," she said.

"No problem, we'll go in mine. This way."

Martin led the way up the street a few yards. Opening the door of a Chevy Blazer, he motioned her in.

"I'm Martin Roberts, I own the realty firm."

He nodded back to the office as he climbed into the Blazer.

"Sales are picking up a little, now that summer's started. My sales agents are out showing property. Mostly to weekenders," he tacked on as an afterthought.

He started his vehicle.

Martin Roberts didn't talk as they drove through Timber.

No hard sales pitch here, Amanda thought, amused. Not that she wanted one. She was content to gaze out the window, watching for landmarks and enjoying the scenery as they left the town behind and sped along the highway that cut through the forest, following the route the bus had taken only a short time before.

Immediately the air felt cooler, the difference between the hot town and the cooler highway due to the lofty trees enclosing the asphalt strip, sheltering it, shading it, as it slashed its way up the mountain.

It was only a few minutes before Martin slowed to turn into a dirt and gravel road. Not so far out of town. Too far to walk, obviously, but less than five minutes by car, Amanda noted.

"This leads to Cora's place. She only has a small house and an acre or so of land. All the rest here abouts belongs to Mac. His land completely encircles Cora's. This road's an easement. No problem getting to and from the highway. It has electricity and city water and septic."

Amanda listened to his description, his explanations, smiling at the "city water" phrase. Well, to each his own. If the folks of Timber considered Timber a city, why not? It certainly wasn't anything like the cities she was familiar with, but no matter.

Amanda wondered again why Cora was so adamant about refusing to sell to this Mac. It'd seem make sense to sell to him, to enable the land to become part of the property which surrounded it. To have a ready, willing buyer, rather than depend upon chance.

Maybe this property wouldn't be for her after all. Maybe Mac would still get it.

"Why doesn't Cora want to sell it to Mac?" she asked.

"Old family feud. Cora wants to go to Arizona to be near her daughter. And she needs to sell this place, but because of something that happened years ago, she refuses to sell it to Mac. Too bad, it's the logical thing."

There were tall Ponderosa pines, Douglas firs and California cedars growing on both sides of the road. A mature madrone whose branches spread across the drive sheltered the opening to a pretty, gently sloping, grassy meadow on the left. Ahead, a smaller, rutted track branched off to the right. Martin turned on to it and stopped.

The house was more like a mountain cabin, old and tired. A chunk was missing from part of the roof near the left edge. The front was faded and shabby. Its large wooden deck gave the place its only attractive feature, yet it, too, needed repair.

Amanda stared at it, intrigued. It looked forlorn and forgotten.

She knew that Cora lived here, but it was hard to believe. There was a definite air of desertion about the place. Perhaps Cora had given up caring, knowing it was only a question of time before she left.

Amanda felt an unaccustomed stirring of anticipation.

She could fix it up. Make it pretty and ... and happy again. A project as far from singing as she could get.

It'd be such a change from her current lifestyle. A new challenge. A pleasant interlude.

In that instant she knew she wanted it. She hadn't seen the inside yet, but didn't think whatever state it was in would dissuade her.

Logical or not, too bad for Mac--this property would be hers if she had anything to say about it.

There were three steps up to the wide front deck. Amanda followed Martin Roberts into the cabin, eager to see the rest of the place.

The living room was a good size, easily half the house. To the left, a large pot-bellied stove would provide heat in the colder months. Near the door to the kitchen, Cora had a table and chairs for a dining area. The furniture was old and worn, the chair seats faded to nondescript gray.

Amanda glanced around, ideas spinning. A few coats of paint, some bright spots of color here and there, would turn it all around. Very little work, really, if the structure were sound.

"Bedrooms through here."

Martin led the way.

Definitely not a hard sell, that's for sure, Amanda thought again.

Well, if she bought it, it'd certainly be all her own doing. She'd have no one else to blame if anything went south.

There were two bedrooms, one smaller one with a single bed. She peeked in. It was clean, though plain. No pictures on the walls, bare floor and dirty windows.

The master bedroom was larger, with windows on two walls, but not much in the way of decorations.

The trees didn't grow as densely behind the cabin as in front.

Amanda moved to see the view from the back. The land gradually inclined upward opening to a grassy meadow. She felt her throat tighten at the beauty before her. The hill was losing its rich spring green color as the summer took hold, browning the grass.

It was still pretty. The quiet offered tranquility.

A short distance from the house, to the right, a bank of bluebells nodded in the afternoon sun. As Amanda's eyes traveled further, she took in the deep green of the rising pines and top-heavy cedars contrasting sharply with the pale, brassy blue of the cloudless sky.

"I like this place," she said softly.

She looked around the room and smiled. She could envision herself living here.

Returning to the living room, she gazed out of the smudged window at the trees that grew so straight, so tall, with dark bark and shades of green. What a difference from city concrete and glass.

She crossed over to the sofa and sat down and stared at Martin.

"Does the furniture come with the place?"

He stared at her in disbelief. "You're serious? You'd consider buying this place?"

He looked around as if trying to see what would appeal to anyone.

"Yes, I'm serious. Is the furniture included?"

He sank down on a nearby chair.

"I don't know. We can ask Cora. Mac won't like it, though, if Cora sells to someone else."

He shook his head.

"I'm sure Mac will survive," she said dryly. "Cora's evidently been here some time."

"Yes, but if he knew she's planning to leave, he'd sure try to buy this place." Martin waved his hand. "All the surrounding land is his. This'd fill it in."

She nodded. "So you said. How much?"

"I don't know." Martin hesitated before naming a price.

Narrowing her eyes in consideration, Amanda didn't answer right away. It sounded like a drop in the bucket for a house and an acre of land in California.

If that's what Cora was asking for, who was she to look a gift horse in the mouth?

"Okay, if Cora leaves the furniture and the structural inspection passes."

He nodded. "We can see about the furniture. I can have the inspection done tomorrow."

He took out a handkerchief and mopped his forehead, pushing his hat back to reach his brow. Replacing his hat, he stood.

"Want to see around the property?"

"Of course."

Amanda rose eagerly. How large was an acre?

They tramped around the cabin, Martin remaining quiet during most of the walk, only pointing out boundaries markers when they reached them. The more Amanda took in the property, the more she wanted it.

What was it that gave her a sense of homecoming? She wasn't even a native Californian, yet she felt as if she belonged—as if the mountains were calling her home.

Neither spoke on the short drive back to town. Martin had a look of growing disapproval on his face.

Amanda mentally reviewed what she'd seen. There'd even been a small stream cutting through one corner of her land. She was already calling it hers.

She hoped Cora would be agreeable to the terms. If not, she shrugged, there'd be other properties.

Yes, but with bluebells nodding on the hill? With a stream running through? She shook her head. Cora had to sell!

Cora looked up eagerly from the magazine she was reading when they returned, still the only occupant of the office.

"Well, did you like it? Do you want it?"

Amanda smiled at her. "I did like it and I'm interested. If," she cautioned, "it's structurally sound. Also, if you'd consider leaving the furniture."

Cora's face clouded. "Oh, the furniture. I don't know. I hadn't thought about it."

She thought about it while Martin took his chair behind the desk. Amanda moved to sit in front of his desk in the chair next to Cora.

"Landsakes, nothing there's worth much. I need to take the sofa and one bed but the table and chairs and other bed can stay. If you want them, have them," Cora decided.

"When can I take possession?" Amanda asked Martin.

"Well, that depends," Martin said slowly. "First we have to get the credit approval, then the bank does the credit check, appraisal."

He doodled figures on his notepad.

"Probably a month or so, if all goes well.

"So long?" Cora whined. "I want go sooner than that."

"I don't need a credit check," Amanda said quietly, "I plan to write a check."

Two pair of eyes stared at her.

"Write a check," Cora repeated.

"I thought the price we discussed was reasonable, but quite a bit to just write a check," Martin said, jogging her memory.

"Yes, with furniture. And I'd like possession as soon as possible, if the inspection's all right. Not," she was firm, "in a month."

Martin was at a loss for words.

"I can write the check now and you can call my bank for verification of funds. I have identification."

She was took her check book from her purse. She took a pen from Martin's desk and began to write. Before signing her name, she paused and looked up.

"I do have another condition, in addition to the furniture. I don't want it to get out that I purchased the house."

Cora shook her head, her expression still one of stunned disbelief. Write a check for a house?

"We won't say a word," Martin agreed.

"I'd like to move in as soon as I can," Amanda said, signing her name with a flourish. "Do I make it payable to

Cora or the real estate firm?"

"First Title Trust Company. They'll handle escrow, though I don't think they've ever had a house paid for all at once before," Martin said, still looking a bit shell-shocked.

When Amanda filled in the name of the payee, she ripped the check from her book and handed it across. Martin took the check and looked at it. Glancing at his watch, he pulled the phone closer and dialed the number of the bank printed on the face of the check.

Amanda sat calmly watching him as he spoke, her tinted glasses hiding her expression.

Cora licked her lips. Her eyes darted from the check to Amanda and back to Martin as he identified himself, asked for verification and waited for a senior bank official to respond to his questions.

While Cora was on edge as the minutes dragged by, Amanda sat outwardly serene and quiet. Inside she was almost dancing a jig. Who knew she'd find the perfect place the first minutes in town. It augured well for the future.

"Hello, Mr. Fairfield, this is Martin Roberts. I'm a real estate broker in Timber, California. I have a check for a house that a Miss Amanda Smith wishes to purchase. I'm calling to verify the funds are in the account. Your teller forwarded my call to you."

He paused while the official on the other end spoke.

"She's tall and thin, with black hair. It's long."

He peered at Amanda. "What color are your eyes?" he asked politely.

With an amused smile, she removed her tinted glasses, revealing beautiful, clear blue eyes, the dark lashes surrounding them needing no artificial aids to enhance their loveliness.

"Yes, Mr. Fairfield, it's her."

He spoke to the phone, but didn't take his gaze from Amanda.

Cora looked at her, a puzzled frown on her face.

Martin's eyes widened and he looked confused.

"But ... No, that's fine. We just didn't realize. Yes, of course. Thank you."

Slowly he replaced the receiver.

"Amanda," he said, still looking at her. "Amanda."

She inclined her head.

"Yes, but I'm traveling, um, incognito as it were for the summer. The last few years have been very hectic. Exciting and fun, you know, but tiring and a strain. I want to relax, rest. Maybe write a song or two. Be myself for a while. Away from crowds."

She leaned forward in her chair.

"Please help me get this a small place for myself in Timber, Mr. Roberts. I'll be a good neighbor. Give me some support. I want to be just plain Mandy Smith for a while. Not a celebrity, not sought after for what I do, but liked, or disliked, for myself. Only for myself. I want to be an ordinary person again, for a while. For a summer. Can you understand that, Mr. Roberts?"

He nodded.

"Martin," he said, as if still in a daze.

"Would someone please tell me what is going on?" Cora broke in fretfully. "Is the check good?"

"Oh, yes, Cora. Today's your lucky day. This check's

one hundred percent good. When you sign over your deed, the place becomes Miss Smith's and you'll be thousands of dollars ahead–less my commission of course."

Cora sat back. "I still can't believe anyone can just write a check for that amount."

"Anyone probably cannot. This is Amanda. I know you've heard her songs: Riverboat Gambler, Sing the Mountain Down."

Cora's head jerked round.

"The singer? Of course. I thought you looked familiar. Your glasses threw me. I've seen your face in magazines. I always thought they'd been touched up but your eyes are real. You're a right pretty gal, Miss Smith."

Amanda smiled. "Thank you. My hair's different, too," she volunteered.

"Yes, I remember it as curly and wavy and sort of swirling around."

"This is my disguise, such as it is. Do we have a deal?"

"We do indeed. We do indeed."

Cora turned a beaming face to Martin. "There, I knew I could sell it to someone other than Mac!" she said triumphantly.

Two

Amanda was awake, luxuriating in the knowledge that she needn't get up now or any time this morning, if she didn't want to. She stretched lazily, rolled over on her side and gazed out the back window. From her pillow she could see some of her hill with the small section of the bluebells, bright and fresh in the early morning sun.

Gazing at them, she felt a warm sense of contentment.

It was hard to believe that, even with all the money she'd made over the last years, this was the first piece of property she'd owned. Shrewd investments, contributions to charities, money sent home; but not one piece of property purchased until now.

She hugged herself with glee a delighted smile spreading across her face. Now she owned land and a house--albeit a rather small, run-down one. But it held charm and appeal. It now belonged to her and her alone.

She'd plan and instigate its resurgence as perfect hide-a-way, use it as a refuge, a haven when the pressures of her career got to be too much.

She was beholden to no one. What she chose to do to the property was solely her own decision and she was excited at the prospect.

Letting her eyes wander around the room, Amanda reflected on how different it was to wake up in this room compared to the rooms she usually woke in. The others had the modern similarity found in all hotels today.

This rustic, shabby room was a study in contrast, with its old curtains, bare floor, shabby furniture. It'd be a pleasant place when she refurnished it, painted and decorated it a little. Until then, it'd suffice as it was.

Hard to believe that she'd arrived in Timber only five days ago. It was a small, almost forgotten little town in the Sierra Nevada range. Its glorious heyday had been generations before, when gold fever prevailed and men spent their time and lives searching for the precious metal in California's Mother Lode.

These strong, rugged mountains still held over twice the gold that'd ever been taken from them.

She smiled again, dreamily. Maybe she'd strike it rich here. It was there, only waiting to be found. First chance she got, she'd try panning in her portion of the creek.

In the meantime, it was pleasant to lie in bed, no deadlines to meet, no new city to travel to before night, no placating her manager or fractious members of the band. Just peace and quiet and tranquility.

She'd recharge, sooth her jangled nerves and try song writing again. She'd loved writing music almost more than performing, but had gotten away from it lately with the hectic schedule she'd been following.

Though, she acknowledged to herself, she also enjoyed the crowds, the applause for a job well done or a favorite song sung for an enthusiastic audience. She'd do it again, but not just yet. This summer, at least, would be for her only.

The sun was well up in the sky before Amanda arose.

Cora Rosefeld had left her well situated—leaving a set of linen and a few cooking utensils in addition to the furniture she'd included in the deal. Cora had even seen to it that Amanda's refrigerator and cupboards were stocked.

"Since you don't have a car it's going to be hard to manage groceries," Cora had told the younger woman.

"I'll have to work something out," Amanda replied.

Surely not a major problem. Someone must pass on the highway who could give her a lift. If not, a taxi.

Though was Timber large enough for such a service? And how would she call for one when there was no phone in the cabin and no cell service?

Oh, well, time enough to worry about that later. If worst came to worst, she'd buy a small car.

It took less than a week for Cora Rosefeld to get the structural inspection completed, sign over her house, pack her things and leave for Phoenix. Keeping her part of the deal struck in Gold Country Homes and Ranches, she hadn't told her friends or neighbors who had purchased her house, nor the terms of the deal.

Amanda moved in on the afternoon of Cora's departure and immediately plunged into washing windows, sweeping and dusting the cabin from one end to the other.

She dropped into bed when darkness fell, tired, but pleased with her accomplishments. The cabin was clean and tidy, ready for the redecoration project when she decided to get started.

But not right away. First she'd relax. She slept soundly, not at all disturbed by it being her first night alone in an unfamiliar place. Now she was up and ready for her first day as a home-owner.

Amanda showered and dressed in an old misshapen T-shirt and jeans. Padding into the kitchen barefoot, she prepared a cup of coffee and some toast.

Breakfast ready, she carried it out to the deck. Pulling one of the tattered plastic folding chairs to the railing, she sat gingerly down, putting her feet on the railing, tilting back. The chair held.

The Ponderosa pines towered over her, rising forty feet or more into the clear blue of the California sky. She looked up at the dark green branches, silhouetted against the pale blue background, swaying gently in a breeze not felt at ground level. A strong peace invaded her. She drew another deep breath of contentment, of her joy in the day and sipped her coffee.

Idly she wondered if the track to her place branched from the main drive to the infamous Mac's house.

How far away was this neighbor, the man who owned all the land surrounding her? She hadn't noticed any lights last night. The countryside had been particularly dark to someone used to city lights, lots of buildings, traffic until the wee hours. It'd been a long time since she'd been so far from the bustle of cities. The silence was awesome.

Another day maybe I'll follow the drive and find out. But not today. Today is to sit around and relax and enjoy the tranquility, she told herself. She smiled again. If her friends could see her now they'd be astonished.

Amanda munched her toast, eyes roaming here and there, constantly discovering new pleasures in the scene before her. Through the trees, opposite the main drive, she thought she glimpsed another small meadow. Later she'd explore. She could differentiate between several of the different types of trees, pine, cedar, madrone, but she didn't recognize them all. A book on plants would be something to invest in, to learn more.

The sun gradually moved from shining its rays directly on the deck now, raising the temperature dramatically. As she took another sip of her coffee, Amanda realized her legs were beginning to feel the intense heat of the sun as the dark denims held the hot rays.

Maybe she'd change into shorts. Sunbathe, maybe take a nap. Good grief, getting up so late and now a nap. It was wonderful.

The hum of a motor penetrated the stillness. At first she was unable to determine from what direction it came, then pinpointed it. From further up the driveway.

She remained seated, she'd change later. If someone from Mac's place was going to drive by, she wanted to see them. She wiggled bare toes in the sun, waiting.

A battered, faded silver pick-up truck pulled into view but, instead of continuing on to the highway, turned into her driveway, bouncing on the ruts, driving almost up to the cabin steps.

Amanda was fascinated. She hadn't seen such a dilapidated truck in many years. It had once been a silvery gray, but was now faded, dented and rusted. It was difficult to assign a color to it. Piled in the back was a partial bale of hay and a tangle of baling wire. She wondered how it could hold together enough to carry the limited cargo. Maybe the wire was for repairs.

It ground to a stop, the air suddenly silent.

A tall, powerfully built man climbed out, cowboy hat pulled low on his face, jeans low on his hips. He glanced at the cabin, contemptuously dismissing Amanda after one glimpse, now looking towards the door expectantly as he climbed the steps.

Wow! was Amanda's first impression, followed almost immediately by, you arrogant cowboy.

He moved smoothly, swiftly up the stairs an air of definite purpose about him.

At least six feet tall, well-built with broad shoulders, muscular arms, chest straining at the buttons of his checked shirt.

As he reached the veranda, she brought her feet down, stood up. Time to make this visitor aware of her.

"Can I help you?" she asked, turning towards him.

"No." His eyes skimmed over her, dismissed her.

Amanda was suddenly very aware of her apparel, of bare feet. Annoyance coursed through her at his look. Who did he think she was? She could dress however she chose in her own home.

Amanda moved her gaze over him, lifted her head and moved closer.

"I'm here to see Cora."

"She's not here."

Amanda didn't expand on the statement, facing him defiantly.

23

"When will she be back?" he asked, fully turning his attention to her.

His voice was low and hard. Amanda had heard of people with green eyes, but never actually met anyone with them before. His were as clear green as an emerald gazing down at her with contempt.

She tilted her head as she considered him. If he didn't have a constant frown of disapproval, causing the deep furrows between his eyes and along his mouth, he'd be absolutely gorgeous.

She took a breath and looked into his face. She'd been wrong about his size, he must be four inches or more over six feet. She herself was tall, yet had to look up. She wished she had on high-heels.

"She won't be back. She moved to Arizona."

"Moved?"

He was startled. Narrowing his eyes he regarded her as if she were something distasteful. "When?"

"She left yesterday."

Suddenly Amanda knew who he was. It had to be the rancher. She didn't blame Cora at all for cutting out like she had. This man asked to have people against him.

"You must be Mac," she said, anticipating how angry he'd be upon learning Cora had sold the place and not to him. Served him right.

"Yes. Who are you?"

"Mandy Smith. I'm living here now."

"Timber's own resident layabout hippie?" he asked, glancing again along the length of her, his eyes resting a second longer than necessary on her thin cotton T-shirt, moving down, ending with her bare feet.

It was Amanda's turn to be startled and then amused. Is that how he saw her? A hippie? Just because she had on old clothes, with bare feet and her hair in a braid? She couldn't help smiling. If Mr. High-and-Mighty only knew she wasn't some layabout. She'd worked very hard to be where she was. Of course, he might not think she had come so far, worn clothes, run-down cabin. She shrugged.

"Cora's gone," she repeated. Why had he come?

"To Julie's, I suppose."

Was that the name she had heard? "Yes, I think so."

"Leaving you here until she can sell? Or does she plan to plague me with a stream of undesirable tenants to jack up the price? If she thinks that technique will work, she has another think coming. Blast it!"

He spun around without waiting for an answer, pausing only for a moment by the truck for a final, disparaging look at Amanda standing at the top of the steps. He opened the door, climbed in and drove off, gravel spinning beneath his wheels.

Amanda could follow the truck's progress towards the highway until the motor faded from her hearing.

For several moments she continued staring down the drive, reviewing in her mind the meeting with the infamous Mac, What an unpleasant man, for all he absolutely radiated sex appeal.

Briefly she toyed with the picture of a different meeting. Her own part vastly changed, the cabin repaired and decorated, charming and attractive. Herself wearing a fashionable dress, make-up flawless—

She gave a short laugh.

His part she couldn't envisage any differently.

She shrugged, turning back to the house. She'd met the infamous Mac and survived. Even experienced a small degree of smugness that he'd so quickly jump to an erroneous conclusion, based on her appearance. Now what could she do to justify his opinion?

Ideas crowded her head as delight at the thought of leading him on took hold.

As she went to change into something cooler, Amanda dwelt less on the visit than on the man himself.

He was extremely good- looking in a rugged sort of way. Skin the color of teak, eyes startling in his tanned face. She remembered how his jaw tightened when he heard Cora was gone, his cheeks slightly hollow, cheekbones high. She wondered if his hair was dark or not. She had not noticed it because of his hat.

His body was trim and fit, evidence of hard work. What did he do for a living, she wondered. Probably a rancher. Timber lay in the heart of mountain ranch land. If he owned all the land surrounding her place, it followed his profession was probably tied up in it.

His attitude needed improvement, though. His constant frown would be wearing. She didn't envy his wife having to live with his constant disapproval.

Of course, he probably didn't disapprove of her.

Quickly Amanda donned a pair of shorts and a brief top. Taking a blanket from the bed, she stretched out on her deck her legs and arms exposed to the sun. She knew better than to stay out too long; the air was thinner at this elevation, affording less protection from the sun's rays. Gradually she relaxed, letting her thoughts drift, fully at ease in the heat of the day. Conscious of the time, she turned over, then dozed for a little while.

The hum of the pick-up truck brought her awake as it raced up the drive. She opened sleepy eyes and watched through the railing posts as it passed. Aware of the heat of her skin, Amanda rose and went inside. She hadn't deliberately stayed outside until his returned. She couldn't help wonder where he'd gone. Did he go by the real estate office to learn more about Cora's disposition of the house? Two days later Amanda decided she was ready to explore her new environs. Dressed in the comfortable jeans and cotton top, she walked down her driveway to the main drive. Left to the highway?

Or right to see where Mac lived?

Her heart sped up a little at the thought of confronting her neighbor again. Maybe another day.

She'd opt for the highway now. She had no place to go and all day to do so. Walking would be good exercise.

It was pleasant walking along the gravel drive, the air clean and scented with pine and cedar. It wasn't as hot as the previous two days. It was a wonderful change from city congestion and pollution.

She pushed the tinted glasses up on her nose again; they had a tendency to slide down.

A hat. That's what she needed. Maybe she could walk to town one day this week and get one. It'd shelter her from the hot sun, as well as provide relief from the glare.

Reaching the highway, she turned right, away from

town, and ambled along the shoulder of the road, exploring as she walked. The road lay in full sun, with dappled shade in long splotches as the trees sheltered it here and there. The day was warm but not hot.

Now and then Amanda heard a rustle in the undergrowth. She'd stop quickly, peering in the direction of the sound, trying to see what it was. The only animals she saw, however, were the gray squirrels chattering in the trees. She looked in vain for a deer. How cool would that be if she saw on?

A slight dip in the highway and Amanda came to a bridge spanning a large creek. Water tumbled over rocks and rushed around large bleached boulders as it scurried on its way to the sea.

She stopped to watch. Its melody was pleasant, soothing. The rapids and eddies mesmerizing. Why was the sound of water so peaceful? For many long minutes she stood and gazed in delight, lost in thought.

Rousing herself at last, Amanda left the road to follow the stream upward for a short distance. She suspected it might be the one that crossed her property and, if it were, she could follow it home.

It was easy to walk along the bank; the ground was not particularly steep, nor overgrown, the gurgle and splashes of the tumbling water a wonderful background sound as she moved deeper into the forest.

The words and melody of a new song began forming in her head. When she reached home, she'd try them out on her guitar. Repeating the phrases over and over, she wished she'd brought pen and paper or her phone.

Still, by repeating the phrases enough, she wouldn't forget.

An entire verse fell into place. She tried humming a little of the melody. It'd work. It sounded good.

Softly she sang the words to the tune over and over. That'd have to do until she could put it down permanently on paper.

As if awakening from a dream, she stopped suddenly and took stock of where she was. She'd wandered a fair distance from the highway. Directly before her was another bridge, a wooden one this time. It looked old and somehow not substantial enough to bear any weight. She climbed up from the stream bank to stand on the planking. The road leading to it was graveled, not paved.

Oh, oh, she thought as behind her came the roar of a familiar engine.

Resignedly she stood her ground as the old, silver pick-up rounded the bend, slowing to a stop at the bridge's edge.

"You're trespassing," came a voice she knew.

Walking up to the window on the driver's side, she replied, "I was following the stream up from the highway. No harm done."

The green eyes studied her. His jaw hadn't relaxed.

"I didn't bother anything," she said quietly.

"Never said you did," was the reply. "Get in and I'll take you up to the house. I have something to talk to you about."

Why not? She walked around to get into the truck. It might be interesting to see where the dreaded Mac lived.

She smiled at her fancy. Dreaded Mac indeed. He was

29

only a bad-tempered, cross old man. Well, she corrected herself, not so old either, maybe thirty-five or so.

She slammed the door shut so it'd catch and they started. The bridge creaked ominously to Amanda's ear, but Mac seemed unconcerned. Once safely across, she looked eagerly about her as the drive continued through the forest, climbing gently.

"You on something?" he asked.

"What?" She swung her gaze to him.

"Meth users and drug addicts wear sunglasses all the time to protect their eyes from the sun."

"Well, I'm not on anything," she snapped. "Millions of people also wear sunglasses just to cut the sun's glare."

"Yeah."

He didn't sound convinced.

Amanda gave him a hard look. The tranquility and exhilaration she'd felt on her walk vanished. Even the delight with the new song.

Drat the man, he was irritating!

The truck ground up a final, steep rise, coming to rest on the plateau before a large house.

Amanda sat spellbound. The house was rambling, with lots of glass. There was no question why--the view was breathtaking.

The land fell away on the far side of the house, to open up a vista for endless miles. Tree-covered mountain after tree-covered mountain rose in the distance, a bluish haze blurring their outlines, blurring, but by no means obliterating.

In the far distance, lofty snow-capped peaks raised

their heads, gleaming brightly against deep blue sky.

Amanda was breathless with the beauty of it.

To the right some distance from the house stood a large stable with two fenced corrals. Horses raised their heads to look at the truck.

She hardly noticed, she was fascinated by the setting of the house.

"Come on in,"

Mac got out and waited in front of the truck for her to join him.

Amanda reluctantly opened her door. She'd much rather drink in this view. It was fantastic. She'd heard the Sierra Nevada range was considered one of the loveliest mountain ranges in the world. Vistas like this one would certainly reinforce that opinion.

Slowly she followed Mac into his house, vaguely aware of music as they approached the door. Opening it, Mac muttered something and strode in ahead of her.

It was the first time outside of a rehearsal hall or review session that Amanda had heard herself sing on a record. She cocked her head, smiling, listening. It wasn't bad.

"Shut that thing off!" Mac roared, slapping his hand on one of the doors leading from the main room.

Almost immediately, the sound diminished. Diminished, but was not extinguished.

Amanda looked at Mac with surprise. Was it the song he disliked or music in general? Maybe just the volume. It had been loud.

Mac continued to the back of the room, pausing to glance back at Amanda still by the front door.

31

"You can move, you know. Do you want something to drink?"

She bristled at his comment. Graciousness obviously wasn't one of his traits.

"Coke," she replied.

When he left the room, she exhaled a sigh of relief. Why was she so uptight in his presence? Granted, he rubbed her the wrong way, but that was no reason to let him get to her. Get hold of yourself, girl, she admonished.

Refusing to let his opinion of her rankle, she moved slowly into the living room. It was casually furnished with good quality, rugged pieces. The upholstery on some of the furniture was bold and distinctive, vibrant blues and golds contrasting with the dark, natural wood. It was pleasant and inviting.

Amanda thought someone other than the grumpy owner must have decorated it.

She was drawn to the window on the left wall. It was large, wide, overlooking the view she'd seen from the truck. Amanda stood in awe.

The distant mountains rose to the sky, acres and acres of trees blanketed the nearer ones. From this vantage point, she realized the land didn't drop off abruptly on the far side of the house, but rather gradually descended until it again met the forest. Two fenced fields with horses dozing in the afternoon sun encompassed most of the grassy area between the house and the trees. To the far right, she glimpsed another barn.

She heard the firm stride of his step as Mac returned. Turning from the window, she moved to the sofa quickly sitting, watching him warily as he entered the room.

He had a Coke can and glass in one hand, a beer in the other. Seeing her, he raised an eyebrow.

"We're inside now, no sun."

He looked pointedly at her glasses.

Raising her hand, Amanda pushed them firmly up on her nose, not tempted by his taunt.

The door on the opposite wall opened and a tall, lanky teenager emerged. Faint strains from another of her recent recordings wafted out.

"Turn that thing off, can't you?" Mac growled out.

The boy looked at him and smiled cheekily.

"Yeah, when it's finished. Who's this?"

He turned to Amanda. He was tall and thin, with reddish hair and pale blue eyes. Amanda judged him to be near sixteen years of age, but couldn't be sure. She wasn't particularly good at guessing ages.

"I'm Mandy Smith."

She stood and held out her hand.

"Probably made up," he replied, winking at her, grasping her hand in a firm handshake.

"Is that what you think?"

Amanda was surprised. Good heavens, he was as bad as his father.

"Not me," he protested laughing.

Amanda spun to Mac.

"Is that what you think, then?"

When he made no reply, she continued, "At least I gave you a name. I don't know yours."

"You do, you said it the other day at Cora's."

33

"Mac, that's all and I guessed that. Don't you have another? A first or last?"

"Oh boy, that's good. So much for teaching me manners, Dad," the boy jeered.

Amanda looked from one to the other.

Father and son—they didn't look it, except for maybe height. Mac was much more substantial, more rugged. The boy's features, while still youthfully immature, were more finely drawn. She wondered how old Mac was. She'd have to revise her estimate. He didn't look older than thirty-five, yet to be the father of this boy he had to be older than he looked.

"My apologies, Miss Smith. I'm John MacKensie. This is my son, John-Michael," Mac replied in a cool voice.

Turning to his son, he continued, "Did you get the stable mucked out like I asked?"

"Yeah, it's done. I'm going to get a Coke. Don't let my old man bully you, Miss Smith."

He smiled at her, swung wide and headed to the kitchen.

Mac put the drinks on the table before the sofa. "Want a glass?"

"No, the can's fine. Do you have any other children, Mr. MacKensie?"

He smiled sardonically. "Mac'll do. I have no intention of calling you Miss Smith for the short time we'll know each other."

She took a long drink of the Coke, letting the provocative remark slide.

What did he want? Why was she here? She glanced at

him again, glad for the sunglasses sheltering her a little. His presence was overpowering. She needed all the defenses she could muster to keep her equilibrium.

Mac removed his hat, tossing it on a table near the door, running the fingers of his right hand through the flattened copper-colored waves.

Amanda felt an involuntary stirring of interest. He was devastatingly attractive. She hadn't noticed his hair before because of his hat. What a striking combination with his tanned skin and green eyes. Did the man realize it? Was he aware of the sheer animal magnetism he radiated?

Amanda didn't like him, but couldn't help herself wondering what it'd be like to be kissed by him, to be held in his arms.

Stop it! She took a long sip of Coke, forcing her eyes away, forcing her thoughts elsewhere. Good grief, she didn't need any complications in her life.

He sat in a chair near the sofa, motioning her to resume her seat. Gingerly, she sat on the edge, conscious of the rising tension in the room.

"I won't beat about the bush. I want your property. I thought Cora let you rent it to torment me, but on checking with Martin and verifying it in the county records in San Andreas, I find the property belongs to you or will when escrow closes. I want it. How much?"

Amanda took another sip.

"It's not for sale," she said quietly.

John-Michael entered the room with the loose- jointed gait peculiar to teenagers the world over. He paused, looking at his father, then Amanda.

"Did I interrupt something?"

"No." Amanda took a final sip, putting her can down. "Your father wanted to talk about buying my home, It's not available, so that's the end of our conversation."

To Mac she said, "Thanks for the drink. I'll see myself out."

She rose and smiled at John-Michael.

"I love your taste in music," she said with secret delight. If he only knew!

Mac also rose, but no smile crossed his face. "Is that your final word? Not for sale?"

She nodded.

"I think you should reconsider." Was it a veiled threat?

"You have such a way with words, Mr. MacKensie. Is that a threat?"

"No, a suggestion."

"I'll keep it in mind. I'm going now. Thanks again for the Coke."

Amanda moved determinedly to the door.

So much for the MacKensies. She knew he wanted the land, now he knew it was no more available to him than it had been when owned by Cora.

"Goodbye, Miss Smith," John-Michael called.

"Bye."

Amanda was a hundred yards down the drive before she realized she hadn't met Mrs. MacKensie. Nor, come to that, even heard her mentioned. Was she away?

Or was there no Mrs. MacKensie?

She shrugged. What did it matter? She probably wouldn't see much of her new neighbors.

She paused once again to let her eyes take in the beautiful view, a quick glance at the modern house, before setting off for home, drawing peace and strength from the serenity of the land she was walking through.

Soon the words to the song crowded her head again. Amanda quickened her step. She wanted to write them down before they faded from mind.

Three

Amanda strummed the chord again. Now from the beginning. She played the melody more confidently this time, sang the new words softly under her breath.

No, this part still wasn't quite right. Still didn't flow as well as the rest. She tried another chord. She could hear it in her head, why couldn't she get it right on the guitar? It was frustrating.

"Hello."

Amanda looked up from her concentration to see a horse and rider on the main drive--John-Michael MacKensie sat on a large chestnut gelding.

"Hi, come on over," she invited, putting the guitar aside.

She pushed her glasses up on her nose, turned the paper over and watched as John-Michael rode closer and dismounted. He tied his horse to a post of the railing.

"I didn't know if you'd be home or not," he said, joining her on the veranda.

He was already over six feet tall. Amanda suspected when he stopped growing, he'd approach his father's height.

"Especially to a MacKensie," he added with a grin.

"Why not to a MacKensie? I only know two of them and one I think I like." Amanda smiled. "Have a seat."

"You play the guitar?" he asked, picking it up and strumming a few times.

"Yes, do you?"

"No, I don't play any instrument. I'd like to, though. I can sing a little. Is it hard to learn?"

"Not especially. I could start you off, if you like. Much of it's self-taught if you stick with it, practice every day. Do you have a guitar?"

"I could pick one up in town. When can we begin?"

He strummed again, then looked up eagerly.

"Now." Amanda rose, came around and stood behind him, positioning his hands, placing his fingers in the correct position on the strings.

"These three fingers on these three strings, thus," she pressed the fingers, "are the C chord. Now strum."

John-Michael did so several times, nodding his head.

"Now," she rearranged the fingers, "Try that--it's G."

He did, his face lighting up with pleasure. "I hear the difference. I'm playing!"

He continued to play C and G, alternating back and forth, strumming fast, now slowly, a look of pure happiness on his face.

Amanda sat back and watched, remembering when she'd first learned, the excitement she'd felt, the joy of actually making music.

She still experienced some of that each time she played and sang. Love of music wasn't something one outgrew.

He stopped and looked up, sheepishly shaking his left hand. "It's a bit of a strain."

"Yes, but only until you're used to it."

John-Michael handed the guitar to her.

"Play something for me, please."

Amanda hesitated. She was serious in her desire to spend some time away from the crowds and people who knew her as a popular country singer. Yet she had no reason to deny John-Michael's simple request. What could she sing that wouldn't give her away?

Dozens of songs filled her head—most of which she'd recorded at one time or another.

She began strumming, then singing. Her husky voice swelling and carrying.

"Go tell it on the mountains ..."

John-Michael watched her fingers as she moved through the song, the different strings she pressed as the chords changed.

When Amanda finished, she launched into a fast paced melody with fingers racing. It was a difficult piece, ideal for limbering up fingers. She knew she was showing off, but couldn't resist. It wasn't often she had such an appreciative audience of one.

"Bravo!" John-Michael exclaimed, applauding, when she finished.

"Not bad," a nearby voice drawled.

The couple on the veranda turned to see Mac quietly sitting on a large bay beside the other horse. Engrossed in Amanda's song and music, neither noticed him ride up.

"Not too bad. You ought to try to get a job

somewhere," Mac said, his eyes holding hers.

A hot retort arose in Amanda's throat, but she kept it in. Blast the man, if he wanted to see her as a hippie, far be it from her to disabuse him of the notion.

She shrugged. "Just waiting for my big break," she said, bending her head to the guitar to hide her grin.

"I thought you were riding to Chad's," Mac addressed his son.

"Well, I stopped off here for a few minutes first. Mandy's going to teach me how to play the guitar," John-Michael said half defiantly.

"For a properly large fee, I'm sure."

John-Michael turned a questioning face towards Amanda, but she spoke before he could say anything.

"For fun, Mr. Cynic," she told his father.

"Few women do anything for fun without it costing others."

"And what's that supposed to mean?"

"Nothing, Mandy," John-Michael spoke up hastily. "Dad's mad because my mother ran off with Cora's son. He doesn't like women much."

Amanda's head jerked round to Mac as his son spoke. No wonder he disapproved, a natural reaction to his wife's defection.

But how had the woman been able to leave him left her baffled. He was one of the most attractive men Amanda had ever met. His rugged good looks were the stuff dreams were made of. His confidence and self-assurance were traits most women admired in a man.

Sitting nonchalantly on the big bay, he was a man to be

41

reckoned with, to learn to deal with, to grow to know and trust, not run away from.

Of curse she didn't know the entire story. He could be mean and underhanded, though she hadn't seen any evidence to support that.

"No need to air dirty linen in public," Mac said.

John-Michael flushed.

"Mandy's not like that. I'm grateful for offering to teach me," he said defiantly.

Mac gave her a long, hard look before turning back to his son. "You get along to Chad's."

Without another word, he wheeled his horse around and rode quickly away, up the drive, towards the large house at the summit.

Amanda watched him leave with a sudden, unexplained feeling of loss, her eyes still on the drive long after he had disappeared.

"When would be a good time for lessons?" John-Michael asked diffidently as he rose and moved towards the steps.

She smiled. "You need to practice between sessions. If you don't have a guitar, you can use this one here. Any time's fine, except mornings. I like my mornings to myself."

"Okay." He moved down the stairs, untied his horse. "I'll see about getting a guitar." Swinging himself up, he said, "I'll be down again. Thanks, Mandy."

She gave a small wave as he turned his horse and started off, presumably for Chad's.

The afternoon seemed empty now. She stared at the composition page, but the burning desire to capture the words and melody had faded.

Tomorrow she'd work on it again but the immediate urgency was gone.

A general lassitude overtook her as she tilted her chair back to enjoy the gentle breeze skipping across the deck.

Ruminating on the revelation of John-Michael, she wondered about the circumstances of Mac's marriage ending. Would she ever know? Probably not. The summer was too short and it wasn't her style to pump others for gossip. Interesting though it might be.

Amanda awoke with a sense of purpose the next morning. She was going to walk into town to see what arrangements she could make for obtaining groceries on a regular basis.

Maybe she'd also get a hat. The sun was fierce at these higher elevations and she could use the protection.

Having straightened up the cabin, which only took a few moments" work, she sat down to make a list. While she couldn't purchase all she wanted today, she could at least determine what she needed and decide what to buy today which was limited by what she could carry back.

Groceries. That was easy. She jotted down things she liked and the things she was low on. Toiletries. Now, cushions or large pillows to use in the living room until she could get furniture. A rug, a few knick-knacks for the place. A few inexpensive items would go a long way to brightening up the area until she could begin the real work of painting and decorating.

She didn't recall seeing a furniture store in town. She'd

probably have to get furniture from a larger city. Time enough for that later. There was no rush.

A radio. She wanted a battery powered radio, so she wouldn't feel so cut off. Relaxing was one thing, being totally isolated was something else again.

A telephone was also required. There was no cell service around Timber or her house. She'd make arrangements for a land line to be installed when she was in town, too. Cora really led a reclusive life, without many of the conveniences Amanda took for granted.

The list ready, she hitched up her shoulder bag, placed her glasses firmly on her nose and set off. It was just past mid-morning. She hoped the day wouldn't get too hot, but knew it'd only be worse later on.

The walk was pleasant. The air was clean and scented, feeling balmy and soft against her skin. The shoulder of the highway was graded and easy to walk on. Two or three cars passed her, but the traffic on the highway couldn't be construed as heavy. Winding down the hill to Timber, Amanda reminded herself that the walk back would be uphill the entire way. Even more reason to exercise constraint when shopping.

She heard another vehicle from behind her, but didn't turn. Time enough to see it when it passed.

It didn't. Slowing, it pulled off the road, stopping just behind her.

"Going to town?"

Amanda turned.

Mac MacKensie had stopped, opened his door and stepped out.

"I have some shopping to do."

"Climb in. I'm going in and will give you a lift."

"Thanks."

No false pride for Mandy Smith. It was a long walk and if she could cover the distance in a fraction of the time, so much the better.

"What are you buying?" he asked as she settled in and slammed the door. The truck started again.

"Some groceries. And a hat, maybe."

He threw her a look. "Good idea. Get a gray one, sort of silvery. I bet you'd look nice in silver."

Amanda stared at him. Could she believe her eyes? Was Mac MacKensie acting almost friendly, almost complimentary? Giving a suggestion in a pleasant manner, not an order.

She was surprised he'd even thought of such a thing as what color she'd look good in.

Her mind jumped to the silvery outfit she wore sometimes when performing. Would he think she looked nice in that? It showed her figure to advantage and was a color that flattered her.

For a moment she tried to imagine what Mac's reaction to her in the silver outfit would be. How he'd smile, take her in his arms, press his mouth against her throat, her lips.

Amanda jerked her head round staring out the side window. What could she be thinking of? Good heavens, anyone would think her a love-struck teenager.

Granted, she found Mac incredibly attractive physically, but she'd been around attractive men before without this reaction. She better watch it. Was she getting bored already? Already fantasizing to pass the time? Looking for a summer romance?

No.

Mac stopped the truck near the bus depot. Amanda looked around, already recognizing places in town.

"My business here should take about an hour. If you're ready to go back then, I'll give you a lift," Mac said as he turned off the engine. "If not, you're on your own."

"Fair enough, thanks."

He nodded.

Amanda's first stop was Chads--Timber's one all-purpose store. She smiled when she recognized the name. This was where John-Michael had been heading yesterday. Checking her watch, she was determined to finish under an hour. Who knew when she might have a truck at her disposal again?

She selected a bright rug and four large upholstered pillows in harmonizing patterns and colors of blue and green. One or two bright accessories would begin her venture into temporary decorating. It'd be a bit Bohemian but, since she was the only one living there, what did it matter? She liked it. It'd suffice until she could start in on all the ideas she had for redecorating.

She wandered to the clothing section. Trying on several hats, she finally settle on one in a silvery gray What a sucker for a man's suggestion, she jeered herself as she paid the sales clerk. Would he even comment on it? Even notice?

One last item, the small radio and she was finished in this store.

Gathering her packages, she could scarcely hold them

all and maneuver through the aisles. Making her way outside, Amanda walked to the truck. As she was well within her hour, she didn't expect to find Mac there. With a swift glance up and down the street, she determined it'd be safe to leave her purchases in the rear of the pick-up as long as she didn't mind a little straw and hay when she got home.

She dropped the packages in and looked around. Seeing a likely store, she went to make inquiries about the phone. She was disappointed to find it'd take longer to install than she'd anticipated, but they'd have it in by the end of the month. An appointment was made and she proceeded to the market.

It was well after the hour's time when she finished grocery shopping. The truck was still parked where Mac left it when she came out, laden with two large bags and one smaller one gripped tightly in her hand. Hurriedly she moved along the pavement.

Don't let him start off just now, she thought, not when I'm so close.

Mac was leaning against the hood talking to another man. With a sigh of relief, she slowed her pace a little. The two men noticed her at the same time. Mac pushed off and came to meet her taking two of the bags.

"Thank you." Amanda smiled warmly in her relief. She couldn't have carried the bags all the way home.

He glinted down at her. "You're late." Disapproval was back.

"I know. Thank you for waiting."

She dumped the third bag into the back of the truck,

not letting his bad temper affect her. She was truly grateful for his help much as he might resist giving it.

"It's a good thing I did wait," he replied, putting in the other bags. "How would you've managed for the five miles to your place?"

She smiled impishly.

"I'd have coped. Do you like my hat?" she said, changing the subject.

For a moment Amanda thought she saw a softening of his features. No, she must have imagined it. His expression was as impassive as ever.

With no reply, he gently took her arm and led her over to the man he had been talking with.

"Ed Tyler, meet Mandy Smith. She lives in Cora's place."

"How do you do?" Amanda shook hands.

Ed Tyler was tall and very thin, with a weathered face and kind eyes.

"Pleased to meet you, Miss Smith. I heard Cora left us. Glad you've come to settle here. We don't get a lot of young blood moving into Timber. Most young folks want big cities and excitement."

He smiled kindly at Amanda, then turned back to Mac.

"Keep in mind what I said. Let me know if you think of something."

"I will." Mac shook hands and bade him goodbye. As Ed ambled away, Mac opened the door for Amanda.

"Ready now?"

She gave him a look as she climbed in. No one asked him to wait–though she was very glad he had.

Fifteen minutes later they were unloading the truck, carrying in the bags and packages inside the cabin. Mac hadn't said anything on the ride back, nor spoken when they reached her place.

He got out of the cab and began unloading the supplies. He followed Amanda in, made two more trips. Putting down the last package, he looked around.

"Looks about the same as when Cora had it."

"I know. But that's what's in some of the bags, things to brighten it up a little, until I can get it painted and get some rugs and furniture."

"Mandy, I want you to listen to my offer. I know from the county records what the place sold for. I can give you a nice profit on it."

He shook his head and held up one hand as she made to speak.

"No, just listen. I also know from chatting with Martin that you just stumbled across this place. I'm sure that there're others around here that'd be just as good. I want this property. It belonged to the ranch one time and I want it back."

"It's not for sale," she replied.

He was stubborn, but she could be, too.

"Times'll get rougher when the mortgage comes due. Work's scarce around here. I don't know how you financed it to start with."

"I wrote a check," she tossed off flippantly.

"Sure you did. You have to keep up with a mortgage. Then there are taxes, assessments, insurance--"

"If it's such a burden," she interrupted, "why do you

want it?"

"It's MacKensie land. My father deeded this portion over to Cora Rosefeld years ago. It was a mistake. I want it back."

"Not for sale."

"Blast it," he slammed a fist down in frustration on her table, "you have all of Calaveras County out there. Find another place. I'll pay any price within reason."

"Another place won't be as appealing, won't have a stream, won't have bluebells on the hill."

"You can plant flowers!"

"It's not the same!"

He shook his head wearily and moved towards the door.

"Mac." Amanda stopped him. "Thank you for taking me to town and for waiting. It was most kind and helpful."

He paused and looked back at her, a grin lighting his face, the first Mandy had seen on him. What a change--he looked younger, happier almost.

"Maybe I'll get to you with kindness. See you."

She remained where he left her, staring thoughtfully after him.

When did his wife leave him? Amanda didn't think it'd been recently not if the lines on his face were an indication. They were too deep set not to be from years of frowning.

Were they divorced or just separated? Had they tried a reconciliation?

She smiled trying to visualize knowing him well enough to ask. That was unlikely to ever happen.

Still, if he were planning to get her with kindness, she'd

try to make him smile more. What a challenge that might be.

Amanda turned to her purchases. She reached up to remove her hat, then paused. Walking to the bathroom, she peeked at herself in the mirror.

Cora Rosefeld certainly couldn't have been a vain woman, the sole mirror in the cabin was the one over the bathroom sink.

What Amanda saw when she peered in pleased her. The pale gray hat was attractive, its silvery color bringing a glow to her skin. Her blue eyes seemed deeper, her skin smoother. Tipping it down over one eye, she tried for a seductive look. Pushing it flat back gave her an open, friendly look. She giggled, tilting her head to one side.

Which mood would work best with Mr. Mac MacKensie?

Tiring of her game, she returned to the living room to put away her groceries, then turned to her other purchases. She tore the paper from the large cushions, arranging them near the wall. The fresh colors in the cushions only emphasized the dirty, faded condition of the walls.

She'd have to paint soon.

The soft blues and greens brightened the living room and made it prettier to her eyes. Two small lacy cushions gave a feminine accent to the rather rugged chair. Lastly, a small rug, to place in front of the cushions and later in front of a sofa when she bought one.

She stepped back to admire.

It was almost like Christmas with all the new packages, she thought as she drew out the Sony compact radio. She inserted the batteries according to the directions, tuning in to a local station. The gentle strains of the music filled the room making it at once more comfortable. A home, now, no longer merely a cabin in the woods.

As the radio played softly in the background, Amanda drew the last purchase from its wrapper, a large sloping-sided black pan, with ridges along one side. A pan for gold--the black color to facilitate spotting the golden flakes or nuggets, the ridges to offer resistance for the heavier metal when the water washed out the sand and grit of lighter materials.

Tilting and swishing, she tried to practice what the salesgirl had shown her, a small smile of happiness on her lips as she pretended she was already panning for gold.

Tomorrow she'd go up to the creek on her hill near her bluebells and try her luck. What fun.

A rap at the door startled her. Glancing around almost guiltily, she quickly stashed the tell-tale pan in the kitchen out of sight.

Going to the door, she opened to John-Michael, guitar in hand, smiling shyly at her.

"Hi." He sounded unsure of his welcome.

"Hi, yourself. Time for another lesson?"

"Yes, if you have time."

"Sure, come on in. I just got back from shopping."

"I know, you weren't home earlier when I came by. If it's not convenient, I'll come another time. I got a guitar," he offered shyly holding it up for her to see.

"I can see, good brand. Come in and sit down. No not there, use one of the chairs; those cushions won't give proper position. Good posture's important. You don't want anything to interfere with your hands and arms. Did you practice the chords I showed you the other day?"

"Yes." John-Michael strummed a few times, changing the chords smoothly.

"Good. I'll get my guitar and we'll get started."

Amanda took off her hat, tossing it casually on the table. She pulled out another chair, turning it so it faced John-Michael, then got her guitar.

"You look kind of familiar, like I've seen you before," John-Michael commented as Amanda strummed a few chords.

"You have, just a day ago. Let's get started."

She bent her head to look at her guitar. Blast, she'd forgotten John-Michael had some of her albums. She hoped he'd just downloaded them and hadn't paid much attention to the cover art.

Her eyes were distinctive enough, even with her hair pulled back and a changed environment, for her to stand out. She should have put the tinted glasses back on.

Oh, well, too late now. Take his mind off it and hope he'd let it go.

"Now, try these strings. Fingers here."

Amanda watched as John-Michael faithfully followed her directions with serious concentration.

"Loosen up, John-Michael," she urged gently. "Enjoy it. Making music's fun."

He smiled, but became serious again as he changed the chords. In a minute he stopped.

"It hurts my fingertips," he said, flexing his left hand.

Amanda nodded. "Yes, initially. But you'll build up calluses, see?"

She held out her left hand, showing hardened fingertips.

"When you build these up, you can play forever and your fingers won't bother you."

She shifted position slightly.

"Now, there are other ways to strum." Amanda demonstrated different rhythms, plucked the strings, and waited each time for John-Michael to try.

"Good," she praised. "You can also use a pick but unless I play a steel string, I prefer to use my own fingers and thumb."

"You have a steel-string guitar, too?"

John-Michael looked surprised.

"Electric?"

He looked puzzled.

"Of course," she replied.

Oh, oh, she caught herself, there's no of course about that.

An electric guitar wasn't an instrument that just everyone had, especially if they already owned an acoustic guitar.

She began strumming again to avoid further conversation on that topic. There was more to trying to remain incognito than she'd bargained for.

Not that the world would end if the whole town knew who she was, but she did want to be just plain Mandy Smith for one summer. Have a place she could be herself, not a well known country singer.

She'd been on such a roller coaster ride of country music, she'd almost forgotten how to be normal.

John-Michael practiced his chords, faithfully changing every few strums of his right hand. After ten minutes, he looked up.

"Now do I know enough to do a song?"

"Sure, let's see if I can think up one using only those chords."

Dozens of songs flashed through her mind, but most were too complicated for a beginner. "How about Mary Don't You Weep?"

"Okay, sounds good. What to do first?"

"G first, then C then D. Listen and watch my hand."

Slowly Amanda began strumming, her left hand pressing the strings. Softly she sang the song, almost in a monotone.

John-Michael watched, trying his fingers on his guitar, but not strumming. When she had finished he nodded.

"Okay, I can try now."

Amanda reversed roles this time, fingered the chords without playing the guitar. He stumbled several times, was late in changing a chord and moved very slowly through the song. Nonetheless, pride in achievement showed in his face when he finished.

"Bravo, John-Michael, very good!"

Amanda smiled at his obvious happiness.

"I've thought of another one, too, Oh, Susannah. Try it with me. Listen for when the sound changes so we change chords. We'll be a duo before long."

"Yeah, do dueling guitars, instead of dueling banjos."

"Or we could do dueling banjos."

"You play the banjo?"

He was incredulous.

Amanda caught herself this time. No of course in this reply. She was more cautious in her response.

"I have access to a couple."

She could call Dave and get him to send her banjo.

She'd better call him, anyway, and let him know where she was and that she hadn't forgotten their date in Nashville later in the month. He wouldn't approve of her being here. He'd found it difficult to understand that she really wanted the summer off, that she'd wanted to leave the city and find a restful, quiet place to relax for the entire summer.

He'd be shocked at her buying a house.

To footloose, fancy free, live in the moment Dave, a house was an awful, permanent, restraining burden. He wanted to be able to up and move when the mood struck, not be tied down with material possessions.

Yes, she'd have to call him.

"Okay, John-Michael, let's go."

They played through the song a couple of times and repeated the first one again before Amanda called a halt.

"You practice those. Next time we'll expand your repertoire."

"This is super. Thanks for the lesson."

He flushed, shifted a little in his chair. "Is there anything I can do to repay you for them?" he asked diffidently.

"No, John-Michael," she said gently. "I'm glad you want to learn and I can help. You come on down any time.

We'll play what you know and learn more. Or just visit, if you like."

"Thanks, Mandy. I'll do it."

He smiled shyly.

For a brief moment, Amanda saw his father's face reflected in the smile.

Mac had once been young, carefree and probably had looked a little as his son did now. It was a pity his wife's defection had apparently changed him so much.

Four

The next morning dawned fair and warm. Amanda rushed through breakfast and her cleaning chores so she could try her hand at panning for gold. She was full of anticipation at the prospect and hurried through the dusting and sweeping so she could proceed.

Shortly before ten o'clock, she plopped her hat on her head, grabbed the black pan and headed to her portion of the creek. She wore shorts and a light, sleeveless cotton top, both in a pale blue that complemented her eyes. Her tennis shoes she planned to take off at the water's edge.

Once out of doors, she slowed down, walking steadily, but not rapidly, towards the creek, raising her face to feel the sun. It was already hot on her arms. She was glad for the shade the hat provided. She'd still have to watch it and not stay out too long.

Amanda smiled with growing happiness at the day's beauty, the expanse of evergreens soaring in stately dignity, the clear blue sky, and the bluebells nodding in the gentle morning breeze.

The soft gurgle of the water could be heard as she drew near the creek.

When she reached it, Amanda paused, trying to

determine the best place to begin. She'd talked to the woman in the store when buying the pan. Basics had been briefly explained, cautions against fool's gold stressed.

When she saw a small waterfall of less than three feet, the water cascading over in a steady stream, she moved to try there. The major part of the snow pack from higher elevations had melted. As the summer wore on, the stream would probably diminish in size until it was no more than a trickle curling its way around the large rocks and boulders scattered in its bed. There were very few spots where the creek bed was sandy, free from rocks.

One look and Amanda elected to keep her shoes on. She had another pair at the cabin and some of the rocks in the creek looked sharp. They were certainly not all smooth pebbles. Gingerly she stepped into the water heading for the waterfall.

It felt like ice!

Well, obviously, she chided herself as she stepped quickly back to the bank. It was melted snow. Equally obvious, she couldn't stand for hours on end in the numbing cold. No wonder so much gold remained in the California mountains. Who could pan for it—they'd get frostbite.

Disappointed at not being able to start, she wandered upstream for a few hundred feet, searching for a better spot, one where she could work from the bank.

She found another likely spot, at the base of still another small cascade, where the heavier gold would settle down to the bottom during flood season. This particular area had the advantage over the first of having a large, almost flat rock near the base for her to sit on.

Started at last, Amanda found it pleasant to swirl sand and grit from the stream bed in her pan, allowing the water to wash out the lighter material, leaving the heavier metal at the bottom of the black pan.

Over and over, Amanda scooped, washed, examined. Endless scraping up of the stream bed, swishing it around in the pan, letting the water wash it out over the side, examining heavier grains to see if they were gold.

Only her tired back forced her to call a halt to her activities. Judging from the sun's position when she looked up, stretching and rubbing her neck to ease the tightness, it was probably well after noon. She'd been at it for over two hours. How quickly the time had flown.

Ruefully she watched the water play over the stones. Tomorrow was another day. She'd continue then. The fact that she hadn't found a single flake or chip she believed was gold didn't diminish her enthusiasm.

Perhaps she'd find some tomorrow.

Or the day after.

After a quick lunch, Amanda again set off to walk to Timber.

She was going to call Dave to check in and ask him to send up her banjo. While she was at it, she'd reassure him she hadn't forgotten about their meeting in Nashville to discuss a new album with their producer.

She already dreaded the thought of leaving even for a short trip.

Still, she couldn't give up her career, either. There were certain responsibilities and tasks to be maintained even when on a hiatus.

It was a pleasant walk to Timber, downhill most of the way. Twice cars passed her, heading towards town. Each time her heart skipped a beat. But there was no gray truck stopping to give her a lift.

She arrived at the bus depot to use the pay phone she remembered was there. Depositing her coins, it was only moments before the phone rang at the other end. He'd be surprised to find her calling from a land line and not on her cell.

Who knew there were huge areas in the state where no cell service could be found?

"Hello."

Loud music in the background almost drowned out the speaker.

"Hi, Dave?"

"Huh? Yes, this is Dave. Hey, you guys, stop a minute, I can't hear."

Gradually the background noise died down.

"This is Dave," he repeated.

"This is Amanda."

"Well, where the deuce are you? We haven't heard a word from you in ages."

As an aside, he said, "Yes, it's Amanda, be quiet so I can hear her. Where are you? Do you realize we are due in Nashville on the 26th?"

"Yes, I know. That's one reason I'm calling. I haven't forgotten about it and will meet you on the 24th in San Francisco. I have a couple of new songs I want your opinion on."

"Bless me, the girl's gone writing again. Yes, yes, two she says. Amanda, where are you?"

She looked around the small town fondly. "In a little town called Timber in Calaveras County."

There was a silence on the other end.

"Big trees and frogs. Whatever are you doing there?"

Amanda giggled at Dave's concept of Calaveras County, the large sequoias and Mark Twain's Celebrated Jumping Frog.

"There's a lot more than that here. It's a nice area. I like it."

"Are you in some hotel?"

"No. Dave, I bought a house. And I have a creek and I'm panning for gold."

"Bought a house? Are you kidding?"

Amanda could envision his face.

Dave was strictly a city lover for all he'd been raised on a ranch as she had. His idea of a good place was the thirtieth floor of a big hotel, complete with room service, spa facilities and an exercise room.

"It's old, run down, off the beaten track and glorious."

He chuckled. "I can imagine. Better you than me. Okay, we'll meet you on the 24th at the St Francis. Don't be late or I'll have apoplexy."

"I won't. Can you send me my banjo? I'm giving guitar lessons and said we'd do something with a banjo, too."

"Good grief, did I hear right? Lessons? What are you up to?"

"I'll explain when I see you. Send it care of general delivery. I have Cora Rosenfeld's old place, but don't know if it has an address. I haven't seen a mailman yet."

"I don't believe it," Dave said faintly. There was a chorus of voices in the background. "Later," Dave hushed them. "I'm writing this all down. I think I have a thousand questions."

The phone clanged.

"Dave, I've got to go, no more change. Bye."

"Wait, aren't you on your cell. No, you aren't. Where are you calling from? How can we get in touch with you?"

"I'll be getting a phone at the house later. Write to general delivery. I'll call you again. Got to go. Bye."

Amanda hung up and burst out laughing. She wished she could be there. The speculation would be hilarious. Probably all the background noise had been the rest of the crew jamming. Well, she'd see them soon enough and explain then.

Though they'd probably think she'd lost her mind.

Her face sobered. She felt a twinge of homesickness for her friends. She and Dave and Marc and Joe, Phil, Sam, and even Evie. Most of them were cousins. All had been friends for years, since they had all grown up together in Colorado.

They'd worked hard to put together the production that was "Amanda".

Except for Evie.

Still she fit right in. Amanda wouldn't be where she was today if not for them all. They enjoyed a special closeness both in work and play and this was the first time she'd been away for an extended time since they started.

Yet there had to be some time given to other pursuits.

Being a country singer was not all she wanted from life. It was an important part, of course, but surely personal satisfaction, a loving relationship, should be important, too.

She wanted to find the right man, get married and have children. Not forsaking her career, but combining that and marriage. Working when she could and maintain a strong family relationship to return to.

She'd thought it out and had ideas and plans for a smooth combination when the time came. Until then, she wanted to branch out a little away from Los Angeles, away from Nashville, back to the basics.

Time enough for marriage when the right man came along. For now, Amanda was satisfied with her career, her new home ownership, and her plans for the future.

She walked back up the main street of town, smiling at others as they passed. One or two looked familiar. She'd seen them before, though she didn't know their names. One she did know. She stopped to exchange a few words with Martin Roberts when they met.

"Settled in?" he asked.

"Sort of." She smiled. "I still have lots to do to fix it up, but it'll do until then."

He shook his head. "I could have found you a fine place, already in tip-top condition."

"I like my little house," she said gently.

"Um. Mac still wants to buy it, you know. Let me know if I can do anything for you." He offered his hand.

"Thank you, Martin," she replied, shaking it firmly.

On impulse, Amanda stopped in Chad's to tell the friendly clerk about her luck, or lack thereof, in panning for gold. She was welcomed warmly and offered more tips which she promised to follow.

When she drew level with Paul's Pharmacy, Amanda paused. A cold drink from the old fashioned soda fountain would be just right, especially with the long walk ahead of her.

It'd take more than two hours before she'd reach home.

She pushed open the door. The soda fountain was along the left wall, a lazy ceiling fan giving an illusion of coolness. The establishment was practically deserted, only a few customers in the store. The wooden floor creaked beneath her feet as she went to the counter.

She ordered a cold Coke, ignoring the curious glances she received. A stranger in town was always cause for comment.

When finished, she wandered across to the book racks and perused the bright covers of the ones on display. If she bought one or two, she could take them back to read in the evenings. Being alone was a fine holiday but sometimes one got just a trifle bored.

Amanda selected three, a mystery, a romance, and a book on plant life in the Sierras. A young girl waited on her, reminding Amanda of the clerk from Chad's.

"You have Mrs. Rosenfeld's place now, don't you?" the girl asked as she took the books.

Amanda smiled. "Yes, that's right. Do you think anyone will ever call it Mandy's place? Or only after I've left?"

The girl giggled at this. "Probably soon as you leave.

That'll be ten fifty for the books."

Amanda set off for home. The walk back was definitely more fatiguing than the walk to town had been.

Still, the quiet and fragrant beauty of the wooded land gave a peaceful air of serenity as Amanda trudged along. The sun was high in the sky, with little shade on the roadside, and no air stirring the limbs of the pines as she made her way uphill.

It was a long, hot walk.

Arriving at her cabin, Amanda's first task was a quick shower. She dressed in cool shorts and a brief top, planning only to sit out on the shaded part of the porch with one of her new books, to enjoy the quiet before dinner, soak up the atmosphere of this little area of the country.

Preparing lemonade to take with her, she heard a car door slam. Leaving the glass on the counter in the kitchen, she walked through to the front, picking up her glasses as she passed the table. Through the window she saw a large red late model sedan. Who could it be?

There came a rap at the door.

Amanda opened it to a slender, elderly, white- haired lady. She was dressed in a cool, lemon yellow dress and sensible, yet stylish white shoes.

"Hello," Amanda said.

"Are you Mandy Smith?" The visitor's voice was rich and pleasant.

"Yes."

"Well, how do you do? I'm Elizabeth Burke. I've come to welcome you to Timber."

"How nice. Do come in. Unless you'd rather sit on the

deck?" The dining chairs were on the deck. Where would her visitor sit if she came inside?

"Not the porch. I never held with baking in the sun. Dries your skin. Haven't changed the old place much yet, have you? Nice colors you added, though. Still, a lot could be done."

Elizabeth Burke entered and made her way regally to the only dining chair still inside. She sat gracefully, fixing her attention on Amanda.

"I confess I was very curious to meet you. I've heard a great deal about you and wanted to see first hand," she said, studying Amanda for a long moment.

Then she smiled.

Amanda didn't know how to answer that. She took a moment to bring in another chair and sat, facing her visitor, and waited.

"Tell me about yourself," Elizabeth invited. "You don't look like a hippie to me, except for those glasses, maybe."

Amanda made a face.

"You've been talking to Mac MacKensie, I bet. He thinks I'm a hippie."

Elizabeth smiled and nodded. "Yes to both. He's convinced Cora gave you this place just to plague him. He's wanted it for years, you know."

"Well, Cora most certainly didn't give it to me. I'm sorry he wanted it, but I own it now and it's not for sale."

Elizabeth's smile grew wider.

"If you talk to him that way, it's no wonder he gets so fired up discussing you."

Amanda made no reply but her curiosity seethed. Who was this woman and why was Mac discussing anything with her?

"He's very upset with your presence, you know. Not only because of wanting the property. You're the first woman he's really had to deal with in ages who apparently doesn't fall over yourself to please him. Plus, he thinks you're corrupting his son."

Amanda started to answer when she realized exactly what Elizabeth had said.

"Corrupting his son? How ridiculous. What next? I only offered to teach John-Michael how to play the guitar. Is that corruption?"

"Only if you're a hippie, which Mac thinks you are."

She surveyed the younger woman. "How did you start teaching John-Michael anyway?"

"I was playing one day when he came by. One thing led to another and I agreed to show him the basics."

Nodding her head, Elizabeth asked, "And you do play well, don't you?"

"Well enough," Amanda replied cautiously.

"Yes and sing, I understand."

Amanda looked at her warily.

"Does it really matter?"

"Yes. I'm chairman of our Labor Day Festival. We have it each year on Labor Day at the fairgrounds. It's our big end of the summer party and hospital fund raiser. Each year we have entertainment as part of the program. The couple we had lined up for this year cannot make it. We just learned they had to cancel. It's late in the summer to get anyone, um big, you know. I thought perhaps you could sing some songs we all know. We're all friends and neighbors, nothing to get stage fright over."

Elizabeth sat back and waited expectantly.

"I don't know," Amanda said, reluctant to even entertain the notion. This was to be her vacation, not schedule another concert.

"Tickets are sold and proceeds go for our little hospital. It's a good cause, as well as being a part of the town's end of summer tradition," Elizabeth said.

"Maybe John-Michael will progress enough to do something," Amanda said.

"Oh, no, we want more than that. Besides, Mac won't go near the festival, nor let John-Michael. That's when his wife ran off, you know. No, Mac won't permit that."

Amanda was startled.

"She ran off during a festival?"

"During the end of summer festival. Yes. Liza ran off with Cora's son. He'd come back that year to visit Cora. It was the year he was one of our performers. We had a small group of actors that year. He's an actor, you know."

Amanda was fascinated. She slowly shook her head. "I didn't know."

"Yes, Liza, her name was Elizabeth, same as mine, but she always wanted to be called Liza. And Doug's Cora's son. They met and his life was so much more exciting to her than a rancher's. So they left together. Right before the show. Left us quite in the lurch. Short notice and all."

Amanda was growing bewildered, trying to follow Elizabeth's monologue. Who was left in the lurch, the program, or Mac?

"Oh, well, that's a long time ago, now. This will be our fourteenth annual event. Liza left at number two."

"Mac's been alone for twelve years?" Amanda said, surprised.

He must have loved this Liza a great deal to have remained single, devoted to her memory, for so long. Was he still hoping she'd return, that they could start again together?

Or was it the other way round? He never wanted to become involved again.

"Well, yes. He doesn't like women much." Elizabeth shook her head sadly. "He tolerates me because I'm his aunt, but he really doesn't have any time for women. Pity, but there it is."

Another surprise. His aunt.

Amanda was beginning to feel like Alice at the tea party.

"I didn't realize you were Mac's aunt."

"Of course. His mother was my sister, you know. I think Mac tolerates me for her sake."

She sighed gently.

"He's kind to me, which is often more than I can say about his behavior toward his boy. He's so strict. I guess it is difficult to raise a child all by yourself."

"Didn't his wife want joint custody?" Amanda asked.

These days it was becoming more and more common for the father to gain custody of his children when families separated, but not twelve years ago.

"No. Being a mother wasn't what Liza wanted. I think

that was the major factor in her leaving.

"Mac thought differently, but who's to say. But I digress. It is this year's festival I must work on. Will you play and sing for us?"

"I might be able to," Amanda replied, still reluctant to commit herself. "May I let you know?"

"Yes, I suppose so. I do hope you will. It'd be such a relief to have that part taken care of. I was hoping to have an answer today, but as soon as you let me know will have to do. John-Michael says you have a good voice and Mac said you excelled in playing the guitar. I'm sure you could find songs to sing, maybe a dozen or so? It wouldn't be too arduous and would be such a help."

Amanda smiled. "We'll see."

She couldn't imagine a small town end of summer party being much of anything. Nothing like singing to a stadium of 30,000 fans and all the work to set that up.

"I'll be satisfied with that," Elizabeth Burke said with a smile.

A shadow fell in the open doorway. "Satisfied with what?" a deep voice asked.

Amanda looked up to find green eyes staring at her.

"Hello, Mac," Elizabeth said, turning in her chair to see her nephew standing in the open doorway.

"I didn't hear your truck," Amanda commented. "Did you walk down?"

He shook his head slowly and entered. "No, I was going up the drive and saw Elizabeth's car. Wondered what she was doing here."

"Well, after you and John-Michael told me how well

Mandy plays the guitar, it occurred to me she might be able to help out for the festival. Since the Renaldis can't come, I was asking Mandy to sing for us," Elizabeth explained.

Amanda watched Mac as Elizabeth explained. Oddly, she felt a little piqued that he didn't draw a connection between her name and the fact that she sang.

So much for her fame preceding her.

Mac glanced derisively at Amanda.

"Could you put on a show for the whole town?" he asked. "Plan it out and carry it through?"

His look suggestion *layabout hippie*.

The last three words brought a determined lift to Amanda's chin.

"Of course I could."

She paused a moment. Don't let him provoke you, she cautioned herself. More calmly, she continued,

"I've done a performance or two before. I play with a few others, actually. Cousins, you see. We have a small band and ... and play for people."

She finished lamely. It was true. She played with her back-up band usually for fun now, rarely any more at a performance. But when they'd started, she'd played lead guitar.

"A band?" Elizabeth's face lit up. "Wonderful! Could they come and play too? Oh, Mac, that'd be great entertainment, don't you think?"

"I think that's your concern, Elizabeth. I don't hold much with the festival," he replied

"It wasn't the festival's fault Liza ran off," she snapped back. "Doug Rosefeld was in and out all the time to see

Cora. Liza was taken with his charm and carefree attitude. You were always so serious. It was just unlucky they went off together at the festival."

Mac's lips tightened, but he made no reply.

"How's John-Michael?"

Amanda tactfully changed the subject.

"Wasting his time fooling with that guitar," he said, turning his displeasure back on her.

"He might become good at it," Amanda offered, not intimidated by his attitude.

"So what? So he can drop out of life and play all day instead of working?"

"Doug was not a hippie. Vulgar term," Elizabeth said. "He was an actor. Lived a rather unconventional existence, granted. But, he wasn't a hippie."

Amanda widened her eyes. Was that the basis of Mac's animosity towards her? Her lifestyle, or what he knew of it, reminded him of the man his wife ran off with?

"John-Michael might become a musician. That's a respectable field," she said.

Just because a person lived a different lifestyle didn't make them a hippie or not successful.

"Maybe, but it's not much of a moneymaking field or one that offers stability or job growth. I don't know anyone that makes a decent living at it, do you?"

"Yes, I do," Mandy replied instantly. "I know several people who make a very good living from it."

Me for one, she wanted to say.

Mac looked skeptical. "I hope it is a passing fad and John-Michael will lose interest before long."

"Did you want something?" she asked rather
ungraciously as he made no move to depart.

He looked rather pointedly at her shorts, displaying her
long shapely legs, just beginning to show a tan. He started
to say something, then paused meeting the defiant stare in
Amanda's eyes.

"I wanted to make my views are clear regarding John-
Michael and his guitar. I don't mind if he learns. It'll give
him something to do. I will object, however, if it starts
interfering with his work."

"Work? I thought he was in school."

"For the summer he's helping me. He'll be back in
school in the fall."

"What do you do, Mac? I know you own half the
mountain and want it all, but what do you do on the ranch?
What's John-Michael doing to help?"

"I raise and train horses. He's helping out."

"Horses? What for?" It was a long way from Kentucky and race horses.

"Rodeo horses, stock ponies, mounted police units." He shrugged.

"MacKensie Horse Ranch, MHR! I've seen your brands on rodeo horses."

A smile of recognition lit her face.

"You have quite a reputation in the rodeo circuit--good stock, fair treatment."

His eyes narrowed as he looked at her closely.

"How do you know so much about it?"

"I'm a Colorado girl. Been to many rodeos there and here in California, too."

She cocked her head.

"You've been around for quite a while or was it your Dad's first?"

"Dad's first. And I hope to leave it to my son. If he doesn't get lost in foolish dreams of being a rock star."

"And that's why you're here. To make sure he doesn't," she guessed.

There were worse ways to make a living.

"Yes. I've said I don't mind his learning, just don't fill his head with dreams and empty visions of impossible things."

He glanced around contemptuously.

Amanda felt her temper rise. How dare he sneer at her home. Were material things the only measure of a person's worth? This place suited her.

When she got around to it, she'd fix it up and make it

a lovely home. In the meantime, if she could stand it as it was, who was he to judge?

She wasn't responsible for his son. How could she help what his son thought, what he wanted to do with his life. Mac MacKensie had some nerve coming here, giving her orders on things he didn't even know about.

She'd fill John-Michael's head with dreams if she wanted to.

Instantly she felt ashamed. The man was only asking her co-operation in dealing with his son, in the way he thought best for the boy. He was probably desperate to enlist her co-operation. Her temper cooled.

"I think you've made your point. I'll keep it in mind," she said.

"Then there is no need to stay longer."

He nodded and moved towards the door.

"Mac."

He turned, raised an eyebrow.

"Could I bum a lift into town in a day or so if you're going in?"

She hated to ask, but she wanted to see if Dave had sent the banjo and pick it up when it came in. She could walk again, but it was a long way and carrying a banjo back would be awkward. If he were going into town anyway, perhaps he wouldn't mind giving her a ride.

"I'll be going on Thursday, early morning."

She tilted her head. "Thank you, I'll be ready when you are."

"Around eight. See you then." He left.

Amanda stood still, listening to his steps on the

wooden deck, stairs, gravel. The door to the truck slammed shut and he drove away.

She moved to sink down on her cushions, still bemused by the events of the afternoon. Was Elizabeth Burke serious about having her sing at the festival on Labor Day? They were certainly casual about things in Timber. No audition, no firm contract, no percentages.

Amanda shook her head. This wasn't a professional show. It was a gathering of neighbors. Would they really want her there?

Yet, why not? She was a neighbor, now. If it was for the community hospital, she'd be glad to donate her time. She'd talk to Dave and get his feedback. Maybe they'd do it. It'd be a nice gesture for her new town. And maybe--

Maybe nothing. She'd discuss with Dave and forget Mac. Hadn't his aunt said he didn't attend. She guessed she wouldn't either if a life changing event had happened at the same festival.

Which it would again this year if she and her entire band showed up. Wouldn't that surprise the neighbors?

Five

The next day Amanda spent in typical vacation fashion, lazing around, sunbathing, reading one of her new books and panning for gold. Her skin was getting a nice tan, the color even and golden. Her hair was turning lighter, too, with white streaks through it from the sun. She was looking and feeling much more relaxed, a regular schedule of sleeping and eating erasing the strains of traveling and performing.

Amanda was also composing. She finished the first song, the one she'd started on her walk by the stream. A few refining touches were needed, but she'd wait until she was with the full band to do that and get feedback from the others in the group. It'd be easier with all of the instruments available to duplicate more closely the sound she could hear in her mind. The lyrics and melody were good and would stand without much change.

She'd begun another song, a couple more ideas buzzed around in her head. Pleased she was again finding composing possible, she wrote phrases and music in bits and pieces. Soon she'd put it together, see how it sounded.

It was a joy. Many of her biggest hits had been her own

songs. She knew best how to write for herself.

Trying the different melodies, searching for exactly the right word or phrase was challenging, something put aside in the relentless schedule of recordings and concert tours of recent years. She was pleased at the way the songs came to her and how fast she get them on paper.

As she relaxed, more would come she knew.

While not seriously planning to strike it rich, Amanda continued to pan for gold each day. It was a soothing, restful occupation, one that permitted time for thinking and dreaming. She'd take her pan and a small glass vial and spend hours washing endless buckets of sand from the water.

There were already several bits and flakes in the vial. She thought they might be gold, but would have them looked at by someone who would know to be certain. Time enough for that at the end of the summer. For now, she was content to think it was gold.

The water ran cold but, if she went during the hottest part of the day, it was refreshing to splash on herself as she toiled in the sun, sloshing, twirling, and swirling the sand and gravel from the creek bed in her black pan. Peering closely as the heavy sediment settled to the bottom. Were there more gold flakes this time? No matter, maybe in the next pan.

On Thursday morning Amanda was ready to go to town before eight ready and waiting on her deck so as not to keep him waiting. No need to aggravate the man. He was already quick to disapprove. She wished she hadn't had to ask for his assistance, but it beat walking. She hoped he didn't feel she was imposing if he were going down to town anyway?

The drone of the truck became audible, gradually growing in volume, until the truck drove into view. Turning into her driveway, Mac stopped near the deck.

Amanda hurried down and climbed in.

"Hi." She smiled.

He nodded. "Morning."

They were off.

The post office didn't have any packages for Mandy Smith in general delivery nor any other mail. She was disappointed as she turned and slowly walked back outside.

Had Dave not yet sent it? Had the mail been delayed? Or had he sent it to the wrong town? Surely he'd heard her correctly on the phone.

Still having quite a bit of time before Mac was returning, Amanda walked through the town to the only pay phone she knew. She smiled at passers by, murmuring greetings to those that spoke to her. Feeling more and more a part of Timber, she was pleased no one appeared stand-offish. In time, she'd learn names and faces and really belong.

Reaching the phone booth, she dialed the familiar number. It rang and rang. No one answered. Impatiently, Amanda tapped her finger against the receiver, but still the phone rang on. Hanging up in frustration, she started back towards the truck. What a wasted trip all around.

"Get all you wanted?"

Mac waited in front of the truck, his hat tipped forward on his forehead.

"No. None of it, in fact. I was expecting a package—nothing yet. Are you ready to go?"

"Just about. I want to pick up a few things at the grocery store. That won't take long."

"I'll go with you. I could use a few things."

She fell into step as he walked. She had to walk fast to keep up with his longer stride. Once she almost stopped to let him go on ahead and follow at her own pace. But the distance was short, the market already in sight.

Her few things filled two bags. When Mac lifted them into the truck, he commented on them.

"Only a few things, eh? What's your heavy shopping like?"

She smiled up at him.

"I think I plan to assuage my disappointment in lots of food. Would you and John- Michael like to join me tonight for spaghetti, then hot fudge sundaes for dessert? I stocked up with plenty."

He hesitated a moment, studying her. Then he nodded.

"I think it could be arranged. Sounds good."

Amanda carefully kept the conversation along neutral lines as Mac drove back. They had a pleasant discussion on the various ways to cook spaghetti. It was safe and would, she hoped, mean they wouldn't be feuding at dinner.

Amanda was fond of her and pleased for Dave in his happiness. The expected child was looked forward to eagerly by the whole troupe. Amanda hoped the arrival of the baby might cause Dave to travel less, as she herself was ready to settle a little bit.

Fewer weeks on the road would suit her fine. Especially since she had her own place now.

They talked fast and furiously, catching up on all the news as if they'd been parted months instead of weeks. Then moved on to making plans for the autumn tour and future concerts.

Amanda cooked the spaghetti, with only a small pang of regret that Mac and John-Michael weren't be there to share it.

Dave stayed the night, slept on the narrow bed in the second bedroom. His view was different from Mandy's, so he duly admired the scene from her bedroom window the next morning before leaving early for his return journey. He smiled indulgently at his cousin's enthusiasm for the bluebells on the hill. A flower was a flower to him.

"I'm so glad you came," Amanda said, hugging him goodbye. "I'll see you in a couple of weeks in San Francisco."

"Right. Take care of yourself. Hey, Mandy." He tilted her chin up gently. "Don't go falling for that bad- tempered neighbor of yours, you hear?"

She flushed a little. "I'm not."

He frowned. "Not convincing. If you do, I'll talk to him. He'd better do you right."

"Yes, Papa," she replied saucily.

He smacked her bottom. "You behave."

A quick kiss, a wave and with a roar the motorcycle came to life and off he spun. Amanda waved goodbye until he was out of sight. She was so very fond of her cousin Dave.

She felt a little lost when he first left, pottering around for a while, nothing holding her attention. Finally, she grabbed her pan and headed for the creek. The great gold discovery just might be today. How Dave had laughed last night when she told him of her panning activity. She didn't care. She found it relaxing and she loved it.

Soon, lost in the concentration of panning, she swirled the water, flushing out the sand and grit, the gurgling of the stream a pleasant melody, blocking out cares and worries. Its soothing rhythm was soporific to her. She lost track of time.

A shadow on the water caused her to look up. Startled, she found herself gazing into the glittering green eyes of Mac MacKensie. Nearby, tethered to a tree, was the lovely bay gelding he rode. She was surprised to see him—she hadn't heard their approach.

"Good morning," she said, standing. Oh, her knees were stiff, her back sore.

"What are you doing?"

"Panning for gold."

What did it look like, she wondered.

"Is that how you plan to make your living here?"

"No."

He waited a moment, but when she added nothing to that, he spoke again. "Did your friend leave?"

"Yes."

Should she try to explain that Dave was her cousin?

"This morning?" Mac asked.

Another gurgle of laughter bubbled up, escaped.

She was thrust unceremoniously back, still laughing.

Mac's shirt and jeans were both wet where she had pressed against him. She laughed at the sight, pleased to see she'd gotten him wet, too. Next time, maybe he wouldn't be so quick to think he could get away with anything.

His eyes narrowed dangerously, taking in her pleased expression. He glanced arrogantly down the length of her, at the damp cloth molding her figure like a second skin, raising his eyes to meet hers.

"On second thoughts, maybe I should forget about the property and take you instead." He drew a finger insolently along the neckline of her shirt, trailing it down to the V of her breasts.

Angrily she knocked his hand away.

"You are an arrogant jerk."

"Oh, I don't know," he said easily. "You felt pretty compliant a minute ago."

Amanda's eyes skimmed over him as they stood there, taking in the casual, arrogant stance of the man, the outline of her own body still visible in the damp of his shirt.

"See? Visible evidence," he mocked as her eyes traced the damp spots.

"You ... You arrogant .. ." she sputtered for words, "cowboy pig!"

He roared with laughter at her effort, infuriating Amanda.

In an instant, almost without thought, she stooped, swept up a load of water in her pan and threw it full in his face, soaking him with the icy spray.

"Maybe that'll wash those kind of thoughts from your mind," she said from between clenched teeth.

The look in his eye made her step back. Was the stream a means of escape or a weapon? Another pan full of water?

"I wouldn't think about it, unless you were sure you'd use it before I reached it," he said aware of her intent.

"I'd be sure," she lied.

Holding the pan before her as if warding off a sword, she glanced quickly around.

"I believe you're on my property, Mr. MacKensie. Would you be kind enough to leave."

Sarcastic words which she hoped veiled her own uncertainty.

Amanda didn't often run into individuals like him in the entertainment field. An occasional drunk trying to be too amorous; an over-enthusiastic fan. All something Amanda could deal with. Here she was decidedly at a disadvantage.

He held her eyes as he answered.

"Point taken, Miss Smith. Though I'd mention to you that people up here are more polite. It's usually perfectly acceptable to cross someone's land, as long as no harm is done."

No harm done? Amanda wondered when she could fully assess all the damage.

He turned and easily negotiated the stream bed, leisurely moving to his horse. Amanda pointedly ignored him, gathering her things to head for home to dry off.

She stormed home as he rode in the opposite direction, but Amanda couldn't erase the memory of Mac's embrace as easily as she should have.

Taking a hot shower to warm up, she found herself

dwelling on the second kiss, the sweetness of his lips against hers, of his arms holding her close.

Her heart skipped a beat. What had started as revenge for her fall in the stream had turned out to be something she had wished would go on and on. Would the opportunity ever arise again?

Did she want it to?

Six

Amanda didn't pan for gold the next two days. She stayed close to her house, as if the walls themselves would hide her and protect her against further onslaughts from the opposition.

More than once, however, she found herself lost in daydreams involving herself and Mac, ending with another kiss. They were harmless fantasies, she told herself, a purely physical reaction, and dreaming about them would get them out of her system.

Probably.

Music resounded from her fingers as she picked out complex melodies from her guitar. New words and tunes crowded her mind and she set them down for further work. She was glad for the time to lose herself in her music, for the time devoted strictly to the discipline and the challenge. The pages of words and notes grew as she experimented with different phrases, different melodies, keeping the ones she liked, throwing aside anything that didn't sound as good on the second day.

She was relaxed enjoying her lazy days, the quiet, slow pace of life. There was a vague nagging feeling of something missing.

The afternoon was warm and still when Amanda tipped back in her chair and reached for her guitar again. Idly she picked out the tune echoing in her head. She ought to write it down. It could be another hit.

But she hesitated. It wasn't clearly defined as the other songs had been. And if the words were what she felt, she wasn't ready for the world to know. She wasn't sure she knew . Besides, as often as she'd heard the words in her head the last few days, and played the melody that echoed, she doubted she'd ever forget. She'd wait a while before writing it down. No rush. It was too frail to stand up alone, too precious to be exposed to critical attention.

Soon, maybe. For now, it was only for her.

"La la la-la-la, Um, mmm," she hummed, putting words to the melody. Playing it over and over, never tiring of the repetition, pausing only a moment before beginning yet again.

During one of the pauses, the soft clop clop of a horse penetrated her absorption. From the sound of it, Mac was riding this way. She smiled with anticipation, sat a little straighter in her chair. Briefly she wished she'd brushed her hair. It look better flowing than tied back. Too late now.

How to play this meeting? Icy indignation? Cool unconcern or tepid friendship? One thing, Amanda didn't believe she could pretend nothing had happened. As if that the kisses at the creek had never been.

She was surprised at the disappointment that flooded through her when John-Michael rode into view. It wasn't Mac after all, but his son, riding his sleek chestnut. His legs dangled down, a guitar slung across his back.

With a small sigh, Amanda forced her face into a smile and waved.

No reason to take her disappointment out on John-Michael.

"Hi," he called as he approached. "Got time for a lesson?"

"Sure do."

Bless his heart, he asked for little and took such great delight in the lessons she gave.

He slid off the horse, tethered it to the bottom post of the stair railing and climbed the steps.

"Your horse? I've seen it before," Amanda asked, nodding to the chestnut nibbling at the grass near the cabin.

"One of ours. Dad raises horses, you know, so we have a bunch of different ones around."

He drew one of the chairs closer to Amanda.

"Been practicing?" she asked as he settled in.

"Not as much as I'd like," John-Michael replied, strumming a little. "My old man's been on my case the last couple of days. "Do this, do that. Is such-and- such taken care of?" Jeez, it's enough to drive me crazy. He's dead set against the guitar, too. He didn't seem to mind so much when I started, but now it's "You'll never make a living with that. If you'd spend as much time on your school work as you do on that fool guitar, you'd do better." Gosh, Mandy, school's not even in session."

She smiled.

"Did you tell him that?"

"Yes. He blew up."

John-Michael stared off into space as if reliving the incident. He shifted in his chair and looked at her. "I don't care, though. It's not hurting anyone if I learn to play." John-Michael shrugged. "He doesn't like me much anyway."

"I'm sure that is not true." Amanda was quick to respond.

She couldn't bear that John-Michael felt that way.

"Sometimes parents and teenagers don't get along so well for a time, but it's not for lack of love, just want of a little understanding. I know you've heard of the generation gap. Some of it's actually based on fact. Different generations look at things differently. It's a function of the time in which you do your growing up."

"I don't know. He's been especially awful the last couple of days."

Amanda suspected the incident at the creek had something to do with intensifying Mac's anti-guitar stance. Mac had asked her to refrain from leading John-Michael on with foolish dreams, but had not forbidden lessons. Why be so down on the boy at home?

She watched the pleasure on John-Michael's face as he struggled to master the guitar. He liked it. It wasn't hurting anyone and she'd continue the lessons unless specifically requested to stop by Mac.

Or if John-Michael changed his mind.

"It sounds good," Amanda said a few minutes later. "Ready for some more chords? Get these mastered and we'll start picking and developing a good repertoire of songs you can play anywhere."

"Good. I'll like that. Were you playing when I got here?" he asked, looking at the papers on the table.

"Not exactly. Jotting down some music. I write a little," she replied modestly.

"No kidding? How do you think up the tunes?"

She shrugged. "I hear them in my head and write what I hear. Do you want to write?"

"Naw. I just want to play for fun. Dad's all worried I'll run off and try to make it big as a rock star." He shook his head again.

"You don't want to try?"

"No, I want to be a rancher like Dad. I don't know if I can, though. He gets annoyed with me so much. I try to do what he wants, but all I seem to do lately is annoy him. I don't know why. But the music business would be too hard, I think. Too much competition, cut-throat dealings. A lot of traveling."

"It has its rewards," she said gently. "But I think you're wise to stick to something you know you'll like and can be good at doing."

"I guess. Okay, show me the new chords."

Amanda enjoyed the time she spent with John-Michael, in spite of her initial disappointment. He was bright, pleasant and enthusiastic. Eager to learn, he was attentive and quick to pick up on all the pointers she gave. They tried several different songs, Amanda playing along slowly with John-Michael. They sang together loudly and with a lot of gusto until John-Michael stopped during one song, watching and listening to Amanda as she finished.

"You're good," he said when she paused, still

strumming her guitar.

Abruptly she stopped.

Had he made any connection?

She wanted to remain plain Mandy Smith. She forced a smile, laying down the instrument. "Thanks. My cousin brought the banjo. Want to see it?"

Not waiting for a reply, she jumped up and went inside to get it. Of all the people to guard against, the one person in Timber she knew listened to her recordings. She'd better watch herself or she'd blow her cover.

As she grabbed her banjo, she wondered if the knowledge of who she was would affect the friendship she and John-Michael were building.

Maybe she was making too much of this identity business. Still, it was hard to break old ideas. For the last few years, the only people she really felt comfortable with, felt were her true friends, were the ones she'd known before she had made it big. Before *Amanda* became a nationally known name.

Still wary, she'd hold off on any revelations.

John-Michael was still practicing the new chords when she went back to the deck. He glanced up and smiled uncertainly, watching her closely as she sat down.

"You want to try it?" she offered.

"No, maybe later. Play something."

"Sure--how about Oh, Susannah?"

"Good."

As Amanda played the familiar tune, John- Michael's face brightened. He softly slapped his hand against his knee in time with the music. From that favorite to others,

Amanda played one after the other. Humming along, but not singing. Finally, after a medley of Stephen Foster songs, she lay back in her chair, flexing her fingers.

"Whew, I haven't done that much in an long time."

"You're great! How long have you been playing? You ought to try it professionally."

She smiled. "I've been playing since I was a kid, younger than you. My cousins and I were always trying to outdo each other. These steel strings can hurt after a while. You want to try?"

"Yes, though just to fool around with."

John- Michael took the banjo and tried out a few tentative strokes, trying the chords, different strumming rhythms. Looking up to Amanda, he said, "You're right, my fingers hurt already. When I get better, I want to expand to this, too. I like guitar better, though."

"Me, too. Want some lemonade?"

"I've got to be going. Thank you for the lesson."

He stood up, a tall, lanky boy. Before many years, he'd fill out and become a man in similar stature to his father.

Amanda felt a small pang. Would she know him then? She rose with him and walked him to the top of the steps.

"It's a lovely horse," she admired.

"Yeah, thanks. He's the one I ride the most. I like him. He's only seven. Born on the ranch. I've raised and trained him myself."

"Looks as if you've done a good job. Do you raise anything besides horses? Any cattle?"

Amanda was rather surprised they had a working ranch. The majority of the land she had seen was so wooded she didn't think it'd provide enough pasture for horses. Still, she remembered the rolling, grassy hill falling away from Mac's hilltop home. Maybe there were hidden acres of open pasture that she hadn't seen.

"No, just horses, except for the few head of cattle for our own use. We provide the horses mainly to rodeos and mounted police."

"Umm."

She nodded. The ranch in Colorado where she'd grown up was primarily a cattle enterprise. The land was different, too.

She'd like to see over Mackenzie's Horse Ranch one day. See the differences in the operations. Learn more about how Mac expanded it from when his father operated the ranch. Find out plans for the future.

Unlikely.

"Thanks again for the lesson. I'll be back."

John- Michael slung his guitar over his back and swung himself up on his horse. Tugging gently on the bridle, he turned and ambled off towards home.

Amanda watched him leave, then turned slowly back to her music. Two MacKensies in one day would be too much to expect. Slowly she started on her song again.

The next day Amanda dressed in shorts and a loose, sleeveless top. Just because she'd had a run-in with Mr. MacKensie a few days ago, didn't mean she was going to put her fun time on hold.

She liked panning for gold. She liked being out of

doors. It was a welcome change from recording studios, airplanes and hotel rooms. She wanted to spend as much time in the fresh air as possible while she had the opportunity. The weather was glorious, her duties minimal while on vacation. She wouldn't let the experience of her last panning affect her going again.

Today she'd pan for gold.

She grabbed her hat and the gold pan and was off. While it was warm in the sun, there were several high, puffy white clouds dotting the blue expanse. A slight breeze skipped across the grass; the air in the shade felt a few degrees cooler than previous days. A cooling trend coming in, she thought.

Going directly to her usual spot, Amanda began the now familiar task.

Time slid by. She contentedly washed gravel and grit patiently with pan after pan of water. Twice she thought she spotted gold flecks, carefully claiming them from the pan bottom and placing them in the small vial she carried.

One of the harmless clouds drifted in front of the sun, shading her patch of creek bed. Immediately, she felt cooler. The mountain air itself wasn't warm; the sun gave the day the warmth she'd been enjoying. In the shade, the water also felt colder, turned dark gray

Glancing up, Amanda was reassured. It was a brief interlude. Already the cloud was moving on, releasing the sun to resume its warming functions.

A short time later Amanda stood up, stretching. Her back ached a little, her hands were cold. She leaped to the shore, wandering a few feet upstream to an area fairly free of rocks. She sat down, stretching her legs out before her, leaning back to soak up the sun's rays. She took off her hat, using it as a pillow, lay back down. The sun was hot on her face, her arms, her legs. Slowly she relaxed, easing the tight muscles across her shoulders, easing away tension. The creek played a gentle music. Amanda dozed.

A shadow covered her face, blocking the sun's warmth again. She frowned a little. If the cloud blocked all of the sun, she'd start to get cold. Squinting, she looked up to judge how large this cloud was, startled to find herself gazing into Mac's amused face.

"Taking a sun bath?" he asked politely, his eyes taking in her recumbent figure.

She scrambling to sit up, feeling at a disadvantage as he squatted down beside her. She put her hat back on, noticing Mac's horse tethered to a nearby shrub.

"I didn't hear you," she said, scooting back a little, away from his overwhelming presence.

This was twice she'd missed his approach. Maybe being by the creek wasn't all to the good if its noisy gurgles drowned out other sounds.

"I think you might have been asleep," he said gravely. She nodded.

"I was, I guess. I've been panning and was a little stiff, so I lay down. The heat put me out."

"Any luck?"

"Only flakes. But I don't care. I love it. I don't really expect to strike it rich."

"There's still a lot of gold in these hills. The mines around Timber produced over two million dollars in their prime. It's estimated the Mother Lode has more than two hundred million dollars still buried in the hills."

"Around here?"

"Here to Placerville and north. You're panning for placer gold. Lode gold can be found around here too, but not as easily."

"Lode gold? I thought gold was gold."

"Placer gold is loose, gold that's been worked up and out by nature, tumbling free in the streams and rivers of the Mother Lode during flood season. Settling out sometimes miles from the vein that produced it. Lode gold is the gold still in veins. In this area, gold is usually found in quartz veins. If you find quartz rocks, examine carefully to see if there are gold traces. Come on, I'll show you."

Mac rose to his full height.

Amanda slowly stood up, a little at a loss for his change of attitude. It had been daggers at dawn before. Now he was offering a friendly overture.

Warily she followed as he headed briskly upstream, his eyes on the creek bed. There was no awkwardness, no time to think about how to react. He appeared to be ignoring their last confrontation.

Far be it from Amanda to drag it up.

She hurried to keep up with him.

"Here."

He stopped and waited for her to catch up. With long strides, he left the bank, stepping nimbly on to the large rocks and boulders rising up through the tumbling water. Pausing on a large, sloping boulder, he reached into the clear liquid on the lee side of the rock. He drew out two white, translucent stones, discolored along one side.

"See here," he pointed along a crack in one rock. "This is quartz, lots of it around here. These veins on the rock are similar to the ones found with gold."

Amanda peered at the rock, taking it from him to examine.

"See the rust coloring on the side?"

She nodded, conscious of his hands pointing out the traces on the rock, conscious of his shoulder close to her own as he bent to point out the markings on the rock.

Concentrate on what he is telling me, she admonished herself, hoping she could continue to breathe. Her heart skipped a beat and then raced.

"It's pyrite, fool's gold. It's often present where gold's found."

Amanda looked around the creek, stooping to scoop up a few other white stones, discarding one immediately when she saw it was a smooth pebble, not the ragged, semi-translucent stone she was looking for. The others she examined more closely. Here and there were black lines which cut into the rocks.

"Sometimes you can crack the rock open, finding the gold on the outside has been worn away, but a bit of the vein inside still has some of the ore."

"Will it be shiny?"

She tossed back the rocks, picked up new ones.

"You'll know it's gold, it looks the same in sun or shade. Not polished like jewelry, but definitely gold."

She nodded, examining the rocks, tossing them away when they didn't have what she wanted.

Mac also pulled rocks from the stream bed, returning them to the water more quickly than Amanda. Silently they dug up white rocks, looking them over, threw them back. Twice Amanda hesitated, then put the stones in her pan for later study.

She lost track of the time when Mac turned to her, hand outstretched to her.

"Here you are, traces of gold."

She took the rock, white on the one side. Turning it over, she saw a wide band of gray-black mixed with a dull metal. Just traces, but he was right, she did know it was gold.

She raised shining eyes to him.

"It's gold!"

She held it out for him to take back.

"It's for you. You can keep it."

"But you found it. I can't take it."

"Plenty more where it came from. I told you, two hundred million dollars worth." He flicked the rock, still in her outstretched hand. "This is probably worth less than fifty cents if you scraped it off the rock even at today's prices."

"It's still gold," she defended happily, looking again at the traces on the side of the stone.

All the flakes and grains of gold painstakingly panned from the creek over the last few weeks didn't equal the amount of ore displayed on this hunk of quartz.

"Yes," he said, "it's gold."

She looked closely at the surrounding land.

"Does it come from here, the quartz?" Maybe they

could find the vein, the lode gold.

"Probably not. In the spring, when the snow melts from the higher elevations, this old creek swells considerably. It's a raging river then, moving a tremendous amount of material with it: rocks, stones, logs, debris. Over the years it washes the stones down from higher elevations, who knows how far. In the late fall, the water's so low it's only a small trickle, scarcely moving at all."

Amanda looked at the water.

"It's hard to believe," she murmured.

Where would she be in late autumn? On tour somewhere? Cutting a new album? No matter, she'd be sure to spend a few days here. This was her home now and she wanted to see it in all the different seasons.

"Are we below the snowline here?" she asked, trying to envisage snow on the trees, piled on the boulders.

Mac stared at her for a moment.

"Didn't you ask about that before buying?"

She shook her head.

"Depends on the winter. Usually we get a few storms through that dump on us. If it's a mild winter, then no snow at this elevation."

He moved back to the bank.

"I've got things to do. You keep on with your search, if you like."

"No, I'm hungry. I'll stop for today."

Tightly clutching her precious rock, she jumped to the bank, turning for another look at the spot so she'd recognize it when she came again. As they started back, she looked around again, puzzled.

"Mac, is this my land?"

"No, your property ends a few yards from where you were napping."

"Then I can't come tomorrow."

Disappointment coursed through her.

"As long as you don't set up dredging operations, you can search for gold anywhere on the creek," he replied.

Amanda considered this, further puzzled. She glanced at him from under the brim on her hat as he moved casually along.

Was this the same man she had met before? The one so adamant to get rid of her, to obtain the property he coveted? Was he the same man who considered her a hippie, a jobless freeloader who should go out and look for work?

Whatever had caused such a change?

Suddenly Amanda recalled their meeting before Dave arrived. Mac said perhaps he could accomplish his goal with kindness. Was he trying that tack? Being kind to her, becoming a friend in hopes of talking her into letting him have the property?

She felt a wave of disappointment. She wished they'd met under different circumstances.

They reached his horse, dozing in the sun. Mac untied him, turning back to Amanda. He regarded her for a long moment, looking at her mouth, reminding her vividly of their last meeting by the creek, of their kisses.

Nervously she licked her lips. Would he kiss her again?

"Look for your treasure, Mandy. What you find you may keep. No strings."

She was startled at his largess. Had she misjudged the man?

"Thank you. I'll ... I'll let you know if I find the big strike."

"You do that."

As he rode away, Amanda felt a small loss.

Slowly she headed homeward, her spirits rising a little as she realized she and Mac had spent well over an hour together with no altercations. She examined her rock, rubbing gently against the gold embedded on the stone. He'd found it and given it to her. It might not be worth much, as he said, but she'd never know because she didn't plan to take it anywhere to be valued. It was worth a great deal to her just as it was.

She dwelt on the pleasant companionship shared as they both had searched for gold in the cold waters of the creek. Whenever she looked at her golden rock in the future, she'd remember the happiness that day. And Mac MacKensie.

Seven

Shopping was becoming a minor irritation. As Amanda prepared another list of things she wanted, she pondered on how she was going to get to town and, more importantly, how she'd get back with the groceries she needed.

She'd have to give serious thought to obtaining some type of vehicle for transportation. She couldn't depend on the constant kindness of others for her transportation needs.

The lack of taxi service made having a car almost a necessity here. She'd look into it further when she returned from Nashville. Dave would give her some advice, she was sure. In the meantime, she still had to get to town today.

A horn sounded in the front. Amanda crossed to the window to peer out. Mac's big gray truck was in her yard, John-Michael at the wheel. He blew the horn again.

Amanda opened her door.

"Hi," she called. "What are you up to?"

"Hi. Dad's let me take the truck into town to get a few supplies. Want anything?"

"I sure do. In fact, I could use a lift. Is that okay?"

"Sure, come on."

"I didn't know you drove," Amanda said a few minutes later as she climbed in.

John-Michael carefully negotiated the turn from the driveway to the highway. She was surprised he was old enough, but she wasn't particularly good at judging people's ages.

"Just got my license a couple of months ago," he said proudly. "Dad doesn't let me go too often, but he's busy today and we need some antiseptic ointment for one of the horses. He got a bad scratch or something and Dad wants to make sure he's attended to quickly."

"Well, you're a lifesaver for me. I need a few groceries," Amanda replied, settling back in the seat. "Are you in a hurry? I won't be long."

"No hurry," he said, concentrating on the road.

Amanda remained silent as they drove to Timber. A new driver didn't need distracting passengers, so she turned her attention to the scenery, familiar now, as it flashed by.

Joining John-Michael at the truck after her shopping was finished, Amanda asked if she had time enough to make a call.

"Sure. Don't you have a phone at home?"

"No and as soon as I get back, I plan to remedy that. The phone company said they could install one by then."

It was another minor inconvenience of living up here.

"Get back? You're not leaving?" He looked at her with a frown. "You just moved here."

"I'm making a short trip. That's why I need to make the phone call today, to confirm travel arrangements.

There's a phone at the bus depot."

"Yes, I know. One in Chad's too, near the restrooms."

John-Michael started the truck, pulling carefully out on to the main street.

"How long will you be gone?" he asked.

"Only a week or so. Would you be able to give me a lift to the bus depot the day I leave?"

"I'd be glad to, Mandy. Just let me know when."

"You sure it'll be all right with your father?"

"I don't see why he'd mind. I'll wait for you here."

He stopped the truck near the phone.

Amanda was relieved to talk with Evie, Dave's wife, rather than her cousin. Evie didn't keep her on the phone long, only verified travel plans and noted when Amanda expected to join the group. They were meeting in San Francisco, flying together from there to Nashville.

"I'm all set," Amanda announced, rejoining John-Michael. "Thanks for waiting."

"No problem," he said. They began the homeward journey. "When do you go?"

"Next Tuesday. Will that be a convenient day?"

"Sure."

"I'll be back Thursday week, if I can get a lift back, too."

"Sure. Call me from the bus stop and I'll come get you. Do you have our phone number?"

She shook her head.

"I'll give it to you when we reach your place," John-Michael said.

John-Michael didn't talk the remainder of the trip back.

Amanda watched the pines pass in a steady stream as they climbed towards her cabin, a feeling of happiness expanding within her.

She loved this area. The tall, fragrant trees, the low-lying green mountain misery, the curvy, hilly, narrow roads. A feeling of solitude and tranquility that replenished her soul. How glad she was she'd found a small niche in Timber.

"I'll help you carry in your bags," John-Michael said as he stopped the engine.

"Thank you, sir."

She smiled at him, struck again by his resemblance to his father.

Deja vu. A tall man helping her unload her groceries. That time marred by the unexpected and unexplained arrival of her cousin. And by Mac's jumping to conclusions.

Even when she told him Dave was her cousin, he hadn't believed her.

"John-Michael, would you and your father care to join me for dinner tonight? I'll have spaghetti. I owe your Dad a spaghetti dinner. We'd planned to have one when my cousin showed up. Your father declined to stay after that. I have plenty for all of us."

"Gee, I don't know. We hardly ever go out except to Aunt Elizabeth's. I'll ask him, but I don't know."

"Well, if he can't come, maybe you could," she suggested. "I'd like to have you for dinner even if he doesn't show up."

"I'd like it, too. I love spaghetti," he replied

enthusiastically. "What time?"

"Six-ish. Bring your guitar and we'll play."

"Great! I'll see you then."

Promptly at six, Amanda heard the truck turn into the track. She'd changed into clean brushed denim jeans and a soft blue top which threw her blue eyes into prominence. She considered leaving her hair loose, but decided against it, too fearful that looking like the cover of her last album would jog John-Michael's memory.

Opening the door, she felt a flush of happiness as she saw Mac climbing from the driver's seat. Behind him, John-Michael followed, carrying his guitar.

"Hello," she called gaily, a warm smile of welcome on her face.

"Hello."

Mac's face was grave, but Amanda wasn't fooled. She knew he rarely smiled.

John-Michael look happy.

"Red wine." Mac offered a bottle. "I remember I was to supply that."

Did he regret their plans had not materialized that evening?

"Can we help you do anything?" John-Michael asked, following Amanda into the kitchen.

"Sure, do you want to spread the garlic butter on the sourdough bread? Once it heats we'll be ready to eat."

A pot of spaghetti sauce bubbled lazily on a back burner, the tantalizing aroma made her mouth water. With all of them in the kitchen, the room seemed to shrink.

She was acutely conscious of Mac's every move.

Maybe she should suggest her guests wait on the deck.

Mac took off his hat and placed it on an empty spot out of the way. His burnished copper hair shone in the later afternoon light, thick and wavy, almost curling where it grew a little longer on his neck.

Amanda knew she was staring, blushed when his eyes met and held hers. He was so very attractive. It was with a real effort that she forced her gaze away, forced herself to remember her other guest and get John-Michael started on the bread.

"I was surprised Dad came," John-Michael confessed in a low voice. "I asked him when I got home and he said yes right away."

"Well, I'm glad you both could come. I'm not much of a cook. I don't do a lot of it. It's not worth it for one person. But I can make spaghetti."

"How do you manage if you don't cook? I thought all women cooked," John-Michael said.

Mac spoke up, the low voice of his son carrying.

"I thought so, too. You can't? And you invite innocent people over to eat?"

Was that a small twinkle in his eye? Amanda felt as if she were again confronting a stranger, not the neighbor she had known for the last few weeks.

"I can manage this dinner," she replied, "but in L.A. I eat out a lot or with friends," she said vaguely.

"Is that where you lived before you came here?" John-Michael asked, handing her the loaf, wrapped in foil, ready for the oven.

"Yes."

"Why did you leave?"

"Aside from the aspect of buying this place simply to annoy me," Mac put in smoothly, crossing his arms and leaning against the sink. A man with every evidence of enjoying himself.

She threw him a saucy look, her eyes sparkling,

"That was merely an added stroke of luck. I had no idea when I bought this property that annoying you would be a part of it."

"Speaking of which, I have a proposition to make to you about this place."

"Oh, no."

Amanda looked at him, her lips tightening. Surely he wasn't going to ask her to sell yet again? She opened her mouth to tell him she didn't plan to sell, but he raised his hand, continuing.

"Hear me out. I want to buy an option. If and when you ever do sell it, you'll agree to give me first crack at it. At the fair market value, of course. That way, even if you're eighty-three before you're ready to leave, I'll know the property will eventually return to the ranch."

She looked at him. "Eighty-three?"

He nodded.

"I know, if you wait until you are eighty-three, I'd be a hundred-and-three, and probably not here any more, but you know what I mean."

She nodded. "I doubt you're that much older than I am, Mac. You look to be much younger than fifty," she said dryly.

He was startled. "I'm thirty-eight, how old are you?"

"Twenty-eight."

"My compliments, you carry your years well."

He inclined his head, narrowing his eyes as he studied her.

"Thank you."

She paused, forgetting the by-play, thinking. From her point of view, she saw no reason not to take him up on his offer, though if she continued the way she'd been going, she'd live in Timber the rest of her life.

Of course, she'd travel as long as the popularity lasted. But she'd always be able to come home between concert tours and recording treks. If she could further develop her writing skills, eventually she'd reduce personal appearances and concentrate on writing.

Maybe.

Or maybe she'd never want to miss out on the exhilaration a live performance generated.

"I don't see any harm in an option. Though I warn you, I have no plans to sell. I think I've found a home and I plan to keep it."

"But just in case."

"Just in case."

She offered her hand, shook on the deal.

"So it's a truce, then?"

"Looks like it," he replied.

"I'll pour the wine and we can drink to it. John-Michael, hand me a couple of glasses, will you. The small ones. Sorry I don't have wine goblets."

John-Michael got the designated glasses from the cupboard.

"To our new truce," Amanda said when Mac had poured their wine.

"To the future," he returned.

They touched the rims of the glasses and then each took a sip.

Dinner was quickly ready and on the small table in the dining area. The spaghetti sauce was thick and rich, drawing approval and praise from both males. The garlic bread was crispy on the outside, soft and moist and garlicky on the inside. The fresh vegetable salad a sampler of vegetables in season.

Once the first hunger pangs had been satisfied, conversation again resumed. Topics discussed were general and non-controversial. Except when John- Michael again asked Amanda what she did for a living. She answered vaguely and changed the subject.

Mac watched her thoughtfully, but didn't follow up on it. Amanda noticed his forbearance and wanted to clear up any misunderstandings—but not yet.

Mac still thought her vague answers were due to lack of a job. She wished now she'd never thought about letting him have that opinion. She shouldn't have been so childish as to try to score a point by not correcting him when he jumped to his erroneous conclusion.

Would he understand her desire for privacy, understand why she went to such lengths to maintain it? Or why she was taking a long break from her career in the first place?

She was conscious throughout the meal of Mac's brooding gaze on her. Tension rose as the night progressed-

-as she tried to ignore his constant surveillance and tried to concentrate on what John-Michael was discussing.

To no avail. Amanda wanted to scream with self-consciousness. Did she have sauce smeared on her chin? Why was he so intense?

Dinner finally over, she quickly suggested they adjourned to the deck for dessert. Twilight would soon fall, its faint light a shelter from Mac's constant gaze. Amanda darted a quick glance at him again, her stomach flipping over as she clashed head on with his eyes. Mesmerized by the brilliant regard, she was entrapped, unable to tear her gaze away until Mac's eyes dropped to her mouth, as if reminding her of their exchange by the creek, the kisses--

"After dessert, we can play for Dad. I'll show what I've learned," John-Michael said.

Amanda smiled. Oh to be young and unaware of the tension in the air.

She was likely the only one affected.

No, a quick glance at the tight clenching of his jaw showed Mac wasn't as unconcerned as he'd like to appear.

Amanda suddenly felt better.

When the evening finally ended and the MacKensies were on their way home, Amanda couldn't determine if she was glad they'd come or happy the ordeal was over. She'd have to watch herself around Mac MacKensie.

He still didn't approve wholeheartedly of her and she wasn't sure their new truce would prove to be a turning point in their relationship. Especially if he still considered her an unemployed free spirit. For a man who obviously worked as hard as he did, she understood his contempt for someone who didn't seem to work at all.

If the opportunity arose, she'd confide in him. She believed she could depend upon him not to tell anyone if she asked him to keep her identity secret. She wanted to clear the air between them. It stung that he thought her a layabout with no visible means of income.

Tuesday morning Amanda rose early. She whisked through the cabin in a quick clean and tidy campaign. She'd be gone for over a week and didn't want to leave her place messy.

She glowed with pride as she worked. Her place. What a nice sound to it. As she polished the chrome on the sink fixtures, she reflected on the circumstances leading to her acquisition of her new home.

That had been a most fortuitous day for her. To find a place immediately and be able to buy it and move in within such a short time was nothing short of miraculous. She found the peace and relaxation she was seeking--and a new hobby. Panning for gold.

She laughed at one point remembering her cousin's reaction when he found out about new hobby. Well, it'd be something she could regale the band members with. Maybe they'd be amused too.

Shortly before John-Michael was due, she went to her bedroom window for the last look at her hill. The flowers would be past their prime soon, fading by the time she returned. Drinking in her fill, she gazed at the stately trees, the drying grass and undergrowth, golden in the summer sun. She sighed and moved away. How silly--she was only going to be away for a little over a week.

When the truck turned into the drive, she was ready. Casting a fond glance in farewell, she closed and locked the door.

"Hi, Mandy. This all?" John-Michael joined her on the deck, motioning to her lone suitcase.

"Good morning, John-Michael. Yes, that's it. I'm only going for a few days."

"I'll miss you."

"Thank you, but you'll have your guitar to practice and work on the ranch. I'll be back soon and we can continue with lessons, if you like."

"Yes, I'd like. I'm glad you bought Cora's place."

He put the truck into gear and backed out.

They pulled out on to the highway just a short distance ahead of the bus traveling from Reno with the San Francisco destination emblazoned above the windscreen. John-Michael drew up in front of the depot ahead of it.

"Do you have your ticket?" he asked, getting out to get the suitcase.

"No. I'll zip in and get it. Can you ask the bus driver to wait for me?"

"Sure, better hurry."

Amanda dashed to the window, greeted the old man working at the bus depot and purchased her ticket. Her goodbye to John-Michael was, by necessity, hurried as the bus had only a short stop in Timber.

"I'll pick you up," John-Michael said. "Just call me as soon as you get in. I'll be here in no time."

"Wonderful. Thanks. I'll be back Thursday a week."

"On the bus from San Francisco?"

"Yes, it gets in just before noon, I think. Goodbye, John-Michael, thanks for bringing me in."

Amanda gave him a quick hug and then turned to climb aboard. She sat by a window and waved.

In less than four hours the big bus was turning into its large, bustling, downtown San Francisco depot. Amanda waited for her luggage, then pushed through the crowd to the taxi stand on the street.

Phew, she was sure city life had certainly become more hectic since she was here. She stood on the pavement, waiting for a cab to pull into the designated spot, watching the busy city moving around her. She shivered a little. San Francisco's famous fog was already coming in and the temperature was dropping quickly. In only a short time it'd be cold and she wasn't dressed for it.

She gave the hotel's name to the cab driver as she climbed into one that pulled into the taxi lane. She sank back against the seat, suitcase beside her, and gazed out of the window at the crowded streets alive with cars, motorcycles, electric buses and bicycles. The sidewalks were full of people--wide-eyed tourists; stoic elderly Chinese women, weighed down by their packages; preoccupied businessmen in three- piece suits rushing to a meeting.

Grateful for the short distance between the depot and the landmark hotel, the cab soon reached her destination. Paying the driver, she glanced across the street to small patch of green in a gray and cream forest of high-rises and tall towers. The few, neatly spaced trees were small and scrawny in the polluted city air. The rest of the view was of concrete and glass. Amanda sighed, homesick already for raw forest land, fewer people and endless blue sky.

Stopping at the desk, she was informed she'd already been registered and was sharing suite 1123. Amanda smiled her thanks, declined a porter's offer to take her lone bag, and, headed directly for the elevators. In only moments she stood knocking at the door of 1123.

Evie opened the door.

"Hi, Evie."

"Mandy, hello, glad to see you!" Evie gave her a warm hug, calling over her shoulder, "Here she is now, Davie, you can stop worrying."

"Was Dave worried? How are you? And the baby? You look enormous! Are you sure it is not coming tomorrow?"

Evie giggled delightedly. "No, it's not coming for another month. I'm feeling fine now, though I get tired easily. I'm not going to Nashville with you this time because I'm getting close to delivery."

Amanda widened her eyes at that. Since their marriage eighteen months earlier, Dave and Evie had rarely been separated. Even his recent visit to Timber had been extraordinary and that for only one night. Now the two of them would be parted a week or more.

"Hi, cuz."

Dave swept her up in a big hug, joining them in the small entry hallway.

"I wasn't worried," he spoke to his wife as he released

THE COWBOY NEXT DOOR

Amanda. "Just wondering when she'd be here."

"Sure you weren't honey." Evie smiled and slipped her arm through his. "Your room's through there, Mandy," she said, pointing to the door on their right. The opposite wall held a duplicate door, to Evie and Dave's room.

Amanda and her cousin often shared a suite of rooms when traveling. It offered a central meeting area for the whole group, away from the public, where they could relax, plan or practice.

"Do you want to rest or something?" Evie asked.

"I'm not tired. Let's go over the schedule so I know where we stand."

Amanda rolled her bag to the door to her room and then crossed into the living room, going to the sofa. "We leave tomorrow, right? Arriving in Nashville late?"

"Right."

Dave joined her on the sofa as Evie sat on the arm.

"We'll get in late in the afternoon so I didn't make any plans for tomorrow. Thursday morning we'll meet with Steve Potlack, to discuss the new album. I've booked a few hours at the studio on Friday to cut one song if we want another demo. Which I doubt. Joe and Marc are already there. They'll be ready if we need anything."

Dave referred to two other members of the band, the bass guitarist and the drummer. Joe's brother, Samuel, played electric piano and would fly east with Dave and Amanda.

"If the deal's signed with Steve, when will we record? I don't want to keep flying back and forth across the country all summer," Amanda said.

"Me neither," Dave gave Evie a fond look, "Especially when I become a father. We'll see how it goes. If Steve closes the deal on the terms we want, we'll be using the studio in L.A. as you asked. It's only if he balks on that term that we have to try to negotiate something else. It's easier for him to come west once in a while than for all of us and all our gear to go east."

"Sure," Amanda laughed, "he'll really buy that one. How often do we drive back and forth across the States doing concerts? It's a way of life for us. Try it anyway. I like the plan. L.A. I could take and not be away from my new home too much during my getaway summer."

"We'll know for sure later this week. If he doesn't buy L.A., well, Nashville's only a few hours by plane."

"I know."

Evie waited a moment, to see if either Amanda or Dave would continue the conversation. When they remained silent, she spoke.

"What have you done to your hair, Mandy?"

"What? Oh, I was trying to be less conspicuous, so I pulled it back. It's cooler in the hot weather, too."

"Incognito's the word, toots," Dave drawled, stretching his feet out and reaching for his wife's hand, threading his fingers through hers.

"But why?" Evie looked puzzled.

"So cousin Mandy could be loved for herself alone and not her money."

Dave's astute answer reminded Amanda of how close she and her cousin were and always had been. She hadn't mentioned her desire to be liked for herself. He knew her well.

"For true?" Evie asked Amanda.

"For true," Amanda said solemnly. "I'll fix it like I usually wear it tomorrow. I'm going to take a shower now. Can we eat Chinese food?"

"Sure. And then we want you to tell us all about your new house. Davie says there's a lot of work to do on it," Evie said, looking at him when she smiled.

Amanda swallowed a lump in her throat. It was so reassuring to find a couple so much in love, delighting in each other's company.

One day, she thought, one day I'll have that, too. I hope. I want someone who will find delight in my presence and whom I'll want to spend my time with.

The words to her song flashed into her head. Slowly she stood up.

"I won't be long, then we'll eat and I'll tell you all about the joys of home ownership."

Heads turned the next day when Amanda walked briskly through the terminal at the San Francisco International Airport. She was dressed in a fashionable denim trouser suit and leather boots. Her hair was gleaming, clean and shiny, cascading around her face, on her shoulders, part way down her back. Skillfully applied make-up highlighted and enhanced the natural beauty of her bright blue eyes.

She carried a leather shoulder bag and walked through the terminal with the confident air of someone who knows where she was going, oblivious to the stares, nudges and whispers going on around her. In truth, preoccupied with the forthcoming journey.

She checked in at the designated gate after the boarding had commenced. Dave joined her few moments later. He'd seen Evie off on her plane to Los Angeles. Scanning the crowd as she moved towards the jetway, Amanda wondered where Sam was. Perhaps on board already.

"Seen Sam?" Dave joined her.

"No, maybe he's on board. Evie get off all right?"

"Yeah. Wish she were coming with us this trip," he said, looking a little lost.

Amanda patted his arm. "It won't be so long."

Sam was already in his seat in first class, across the aisle from the two booked for Amanda and Dave. He greeted them, indicating he'd trade places with Dave later in the flight to spend some of the travel time with Amanda.

It was a long, boring flight. Amanda had made it several times in the last few years, always on business. She talked part of the time with her cousin, part of the time with Sam, to catch up on family news, go over some of the business that had cropped up in her absence.

Dave brought up business first. They discussed the forthcoming meeting in further detail and the possibilities it opened, the terms they wanted and some of the possible songs for the new album. Dave complimented Amanda on the songs she'd most recently written. The ones she'd sent to him had been tried with the band and both had sounded good.

"What about your rancher?" he asked next.

"What about him?" she asked.

Mac wasn't precisely *her* rancher.

"I'm asking you that. You tell me."

"He's not my rancher, as you put it."

"Do you want him to be?"

Amanda was silent a long time, staring out the window at the empty sky.

"I'm not sure," she answered slowly. " I find him very attractive, very sexy. I like being around him, but he's so hard to get to know. It's early days so maybe there's a chance we can get to know each other better. I'm sure willing."

She was silent for a moment in thought.

"I want to get married some day if I can find someone to have a very special relationship with. To love, to have love me." She smiled at Dave. "Like you and Evie."

"And give up all this?" He waved his hand.

"No, not all. I don't think I'll want to travel as much in the future. It gets tiring. But I don't want to give it up totally. Only not so much. That's not so outrageous, is it?"

"I could handle that, especially with a kid in the family. Evie won't be able to travel with me as much."

"I could spend more time writing songs. I really like that part, Davie."

"It's where you started, what you're good at. In addition to the singing, of course. But the rancher?"

"I don't know."

Suddenly the kisses by the stream flashed into her mind. She'd like to get to know Mac better. But she didn't pin hopes for a long-lasting relationship on someone who treated her like he did, no matter how attracted he was physically.

There had to be more than sexual attraction to forge a

lasting bond.

She shrugged. "Time will tell, I guess. What are we doing for the album?"

"We want to include the ones you just wrote. They should both go. Bluebells on the Hills is the one that needs a little more work."

"Yes, I know. I thought it'd help to hear it with the band. Maybe I can better figure out where it's weak."

"Lyrics are nice."

She bowed her head slightly, her smile heartfelt.

"Thanks, cuz. I think I'm ready to settle down."

"So your song says. Me, too." Dave was silent for a moment. "It's been grand fun, though."

"Sure, and will still be, only not so much travel."

The big plane droned on, flying eastward towards the Great Smokey mountains of Tennessee, and country music's home in Nashville.

Dave swapped seats with Sam. He and Amanda flew the last hour together, catching up on family. Sam had taken a few weeks to visit Colorado and was bringing Amanda up to date on everything and everyone from their home town.

Joe and Marc met the plane, greeting the travelers, taking them to the hotel where they had already reserved rooms. It was located near the famous Renshaw Theater, first home of the Grand Ole Opry.

Amanda didn't even notice the city as they drove through it. She'd been here many times now and no longer stood in awe. She was here to do a job. Work and then go home. She had neither the time nor inclination for tourism.

Eight

Amanda was tired but felt the stirring of excitement as the bus drew near Timber. Her trip had been short and hectic, not the least of which had been this final leg. Up early yesterday to fly from Nashville to Los Angeles.

Making arrangements to have some furniture shipped from L.A. to her cabin had kept her busy in the afternoon. Then, up early again this morning to catch the flight to San Francisco in time to connect with the bus.

What with the time zone differences, irregular meals and the heavy schedule in Nashville, she was worn out. She hoped John-Michael would pick her up as soon as she called.

She was still attired as she had been for the last week; hair freshly washed, wavy and soft in the bright sun, make-up tastefully applied. Her dark blue denim trouser suit was not suitable for summer traveling in California's hot central valley, but had been welcomed for San Francisco's cool, foggy climate and wouldn't be too heavy for the cooler mountain air. When she took off the jacket, it looked like jeans and a cool blouse. Fortunately, the bus was air-conditioned.

Familiar landmarks sparked recognition. She recalled this stretch of highway. Soon they'd round a bend, see the river and traverse the bridge. Next stop, Timber.

As they pulled into the gas station and bus depot, Amanda saw the gray truck parked near the building. John-Michael must have checked the bus schedule. Grateful she didn't have to wait at all, she gather her few things from her seat. The teenager stood by the truck, waiting. Almost home now.

When she stepped from the vehicle, her heart caught in her throat. Mac MacKensie was the person leaning back against the hood of the battered old truck, hat low on his face, arms crossed. It wasn't John-Michael after all.

Her heart rate increased at the sight of him. She smiled as she walked over as casually as she could. Her first inclination had been to hurry to see him.

"Hi."

Was that breathless voice hers? She had enough carrying power to be heard at the back of an auditorium without a mike if needed.

"Have a good trip?"

He took in her appearance, his eyes wandering slowly from her hair to her fancy boots.

"Yes, thanks."

He glanced at her face.

"Come into an inheritance?"

"No. Is, uh, did John-Michael come?"

"Nope. I'll give you a lift home."

"Thank you. I have a few more cases this time."

He shrugged and moved to open the door.

"Climb in and I'll get them. You're the only one off the bus, I take it all the baggage will be yours."

Glancing back, Amanda realized the driver was already unloading her things from the luggage area. Every box and bag looked familiar.

"It looks like it. I'll help."

"I can manage. Just get in."

"Yes, sir!"

She gave a mock salute, stopping Mac in his tracks as he turned towards the bus.

When he glared at her, Amanda giggled, gave a saucy wink and promptly climbed into the cab.

She watched as Mac gathered all the boxes and bag and loaded them in the truck. Her eyes feasted on him. She'd almost forgotten how tall he was, how broad his shoulders were. His hat, pulled low on his forehead, hid most of the bronzed hair, though she could see a bit when his back was to her.

He was certainly an attractive man, in spite of the stern expression he perpetually wore. She remembered how he looked when he smiled. He should do it more often.

When the last box had been placed in the truck, he joined her in the cab, the look from his green eyes almost like an electric shock. He stared her for a long, charged moment, at last moving to start the engine.

"You look nice," he said, turning the wheel to take the pickup from the parking lot. "A little tired, though."

"I am tired," she replied. "Thank you for picking me up. Where's John-Michael?"

"Home."

"Was it inconvenient for him to come for me?"

Mac threw her a look. "Object to me?"

"No, of course not. I just... I mean I was expecting John-Michael."

What was the matter with her? She had just negotiated and signed a large recording contract; started preliminaries plans for a concert tour in the autumn; traveled across the country and back; made arrangements to have furniture delivered and was now stammering like a teenager. Taking a deep breath, she slowly released it.

"I had to come to town, so I picked you up. I wanted to see you."

Amanda's heart gave a small skip. Mac had wanted to see her. Her face broke into a lovely smile as she shifted a little in the seat, relaxing a little.

He spoke again. "Why so much stuff this time? You hit a jackpot or something?"

"No. I have an apartment in L.A. and I'm bringing things back here to really make my cabin a home. I was only planning to check out the area when I came before. Then I saw Cora's place and stayed."

"Without further investigation?"

He looked disapproving.

She shrugged. "It was a wild splurge. I saw something I liked and bought it. Haven't you ever done anything like that?"

"What if you didn't like it here? What if you found it was a mistake to move to Timber? Did you consider that?"

"Nope, not at all. If I don't like it, I'll leave. I can always change my mind. I'm not hurting anyone. Not responsible to anyone for how I live my life. I certainly won't do or not do something because of other people's views."

"Free spirited people always see themselves as beholden to no one. Live their lives however they choose. Irresponsible, that's all," Mac said.

"Others choose to live their lives as they want. All people who are working at something they like, who live where they want, are doing the same thing. That doesn't make them irresponsible. Aren't you glad you're a rancher?"

"Of course I am. But I didn't buy a place on impulse without checking into it."

"But I did," she replied sweetly, "and I'll do it again if I choose."

"Oh, so we're rich now, are we? Where are you buying your next place?"

"I'd do it all over again here," she rephrased. "Why did you want to see me?"

"I came to see you last Thursday. I didn't realize you'd gone anywhere. John-Michael didn't mention it until I asked him. I have that option agreement we discussed."

Amanda felt like a pricked balloon. He only wanted to see her so they could lock in the option agreement. He hadn't really wanted to see her today except to ensure his hold on her property.

She was so disappointed she wanted to cry. She was tempted to renege on the option and let him worry if she'd ever sell to him or not. More fool her for thinking he wanted to see her for any reason other than business. Well, so be it.

"Fine. I'll look at it," she said, fatigue sweeping

through. She fell silent for the remainder of the ride.

In spite of her disappointment, when they rounded the bend to her track, she felt a lifting of spirits. Her cabin looked so small and isolated after the massive, crowded high-rises and glass building of the cities.

The soaring pines, the brown grassy meadows, the quiet breeze were soothing to jangled nerves, sweeping through her with a sense of tranquility.

Amanda was glad to be home. To be home with no reason to go away again until the summer was over. She'd spend the weeks ahead decorating and writing songs. It'd be a wonderful summer and she "d enjoy every minute of it.

In spite of her disapproving neighbor.

As soon as Mac stopped, Amanda climbed out, going to the back of the truck and pulling one of her cases from it.

"I will get those," Mac said coming around and lifting two other cases.

"I can help," she said, heading for the door.

Once unlocked, Amanda carried her case directly through to her bedroom. She flung open the window, silently greeting the hills, the trees, and her bluebells now waning.

When she re-entered the living room a few moments later, Mac was setting down the last of her baggage.

Crossing to the front window, she opened it for cross-ventilation. Taking off her jacket, she laid it and her sun-glasses on the table.

"Did you get a job?" Mac asked, watching her.

"I may have something lined up for the fall," she replied, shrugging.

"I wondered, you look all fixed up. For an interview?"

Amanda's hackles rose again. She'd forgotten for a moment he thought her a out-of-work free spirit. It was such a different impression from what most people thought about her.

An imp of mischief took over. Giving him a big grin, she turned around.

"Do you like it? I bought some other things, too, now that I'm moving in for good."

She opened her eyes wide and stared up at him.

"Where did you get the money for all this finery?"

"Here and there."

She waved her hand vaguely.

"Doing something you shouldn't, I warrant. Did it involve that biker dude you had spend the night a while back?"

"Biker dud? You mean Dave?" Amanda gave a small giggle. "Dave's not a biker. He's my cousin."

"I bet!"

"Where's the option agreement?"

She changed the subject before she got mad again.

"Here."

Mac drew an envelope from his pocket and handed it to her.

Amanda opened it and scanned the page. It looked pretty standard to her, but she'd read it carefully before signing. The amount for purchase of the option was blank. She looked up questioningly.

"We never discussed money. My attorney drew up the agreement and left that blank. There should be some remittance for the option. How much?" Mac asked.

Still piqued that he'd only come for her to clear up the option, she replied carelessly, "Five thousand."

"You're nuts!" he thundered. "I'm not paying for your life here in Timber! You find your income somewhere else. You want a job, I'll help you get one, but you're not coasting free on my money."

Amanda smiled. My, he was quick-tempered. Could she always make him mad so easily she wondered, tilting her head as she looked at him.

"Too high, eh?"

"You know it is. I say one hundred dollars."

"Fine" she replied instantly, amiably.

Mac stared at her a long moment, reading the laughter in her eyes.

Slowly relaxing until the glimmer of a smile touched his lips.

"I'll read the agreement tonight and bring it up to your place tomorrow. I'm tired and want to eat and go to bed."

"All right. Fair enough. I'll be home in the morning."

"Thanks again for bringing me home. I guess I'm going to have to get a car or something. This place is just too far to walk to town for everything."

"Before I forget, Elizabeth instructed me to invite you for dinner next Wednesday. She's having a few people in and wanted you to join them."

"Where does she live?"

"Not too far from here. I can give you a lift. John-

Michael and I are going, too. No trouble."

Amanda nodded, certain Mac wouldn't have offered if it was inconvenient.

"Do you have a, uh ... dress?" he asked.

"Yes, of course." She gave him an exasperated look. "Don't you worry, I won't let your aunt down. What time?"

"About seven. We'll be by a little before."

"That'll work. Tell John-Michael hi for me, will you?"

"Yes."

Mac turned, pulled his hat down firmly and opened the door, pausing to throw a glance back at Amanda. "Glad you're back, spitfire."

"I'll bet," she mimicked.

Up early the next morning, Amanda waited until after ten before walking up to Mac's home to give him the signed option agreement. She'd read it carefully the night before. It was clear-cut and straightforward--if and when she ever sold the property, in exchange for the $100 Mac'd give her, she'd give him first right of refusal to buy the property at the then fair market value.

Amanda saw nothing wrong with it, signed it and was now carrying it to return to Mac. The gravel roadway wound upward through the tall trees.

Rustlings in the undergrowth and the birds chirping their own melodies reminded Amanda she was not alone on her walk, even though she didn't see another creature. What a pleasant way of life. She liked cities for the cultural advantages they offered, but she loved the country.

The wooden bridge traversing the creek didn't seem any more substantial to Amanda than it had before. She walked quickly across it, watching her step. Shaky though it appeared, it was solid and didn't move at all under her slight weight. That obstacle behind her, she continued briskly up the drive.

She was dressed in her inevitable jeans and T-shirt, hair drawn back in a ribbon and glasses firmly in position. Since she'd received a reprieve yesterday with Mac picking her up instead of John-Michael, she'd decided not to tempt fate. Her disguise, such as it was, was back in place.

Cresting the last hill, Amanda paused as she again took in the view from the home site. The endless mountains rising in the distance looked a little blurry today. To the left, in the far distance, a stately snow-capped peak rose loftily above the tree line. Amanda gazed out for endless moments, spellbound by the sheer beauty of the view.

Slowly she turned towards the house. It was in a wonderful location. The barn discretely away enough not to feel like it crowded the open space. If it were hers, she'd spend hours on the deck, just staring out over the land. Did Mac ever do that?

Did he share any of her feelings about the mountains being special? Or just take it all for granted, never consciously aware of the sheer beauty, the mighty majesty of the Sierra Nevada range?

Mac answered the door. There was no loud music blaring this time, only the soft swish of the breeze through the grass and trees.

"Hello."

His look quickly took in her attire.

"Hi. I brought the option letter."

"Back to mountain dress, I see," he commented.

She shrugged. "It's comfy. Do I come in or just hand it over to you and leave?"

She offered the paper.

Stepping aside, he opened the door wider. As she passed by, he took the paper, opening it and verifying she'd signed. He closed the door watching Amanda closely.

She felt her pulse quicken with the sound of the latch. She was in Mac's house on the hill. Alone?

"Where's John-Michael?" she asked, in what she hoped was a casual tone.

"Down at the barn. You walked up?"

"Of course."

She took off her glasses and moved to the large window. The view was even better from this position.

"Thought maybe your friend from the other night might have given you a lift."

"Dave? He doesn't live around here."

"Did you see him on your trip?" Mac left the door to join her near the window.

"We traveled together."

"I bet you did."

Amanda felt the tug at the back of her head, then her hair fell free onto her shoulders. She spun round to find herself very close to Mac. He was dangling the ribbon.

"Give it back," she said, her heart starting to pound.

"Why not leave it down? It looks nice that way." he said, his fingers already brushing through.

"It's too hot."

She reached for the ribbon, but he dangled it away

133

from her with his other hand.

"It's not hot in here. Pleasant, I thought."

"Come on, Mac."

"Come and get it," he invited softy.

Amanda glared at him a moment, then put on a deliberately sweet expression, moving close to him, looking up nicely into his face, eyes blazing.

"Please Mac, give my ribbon to me," she said as sweetly as she knew how..

He smiled. "How artificial."

Moving quickly, he pulled her into his arms, his face blotting out all else as his mouth claimed hers.

Amanda was startled, not expecting his embrace. Before she could protest, however, his arms pulled her against him, molding her body to his, his lips warm and persuasive against hers, the contact with his body sending waves of desire and longing through her.

One touch of his mouth and she was lost.

As the kiss deepened, Amanda was vaguely aware of Mac's hand in her hair, running his fingers through the long tresses, gently rubbing the nape of her neck. She shivered with delight, floating on waves of sweet pleasure.

Her heart began beating heavily as she grew breathless with the feelings Mac could evoke. She moved closer still, pressing against him, moving easily in his arms as he tilted her head back and trailed kisses down her throat, back to her mouth.

His hands warm and gentle in her hair, rubbing her back, tracing her spine, up and down.

Amanda's arms locked together around his neck as she

tried to slow the fire building within her. His mouth hot and sweet against hers. The moments floated by.

Suddenly Mac broke away.

At the same second, Amanda heard a familiar voice.

"Dad." John-Michael entered the room from the front door, surprise held him silent only a moment, then a big grin lit his face.

"Hi, Mandy. I see you're back."

Blushing like a schoolgirl, she tried a weak smile.

"Hi, John-Michael. Yes, I'm back."

She didn't look at Mac. In fact, Amanda didn't know where to look. Maybe she could just jump out of the window and end it all.

Mac moved to his desk and rummaged through some papers.

"I believe I owe you a check."

"Wow, Mandy, you must be good!" John-Michael teased, laughing as she blushed again.

"John-Michael!" Mac's voice was thunderous.

"Yeah?" He was still smiling.

"What are you doing here?"

"I live here."

"Don't get smart. I mean now. I thought you were going to exercise the two horses."

"That's why I'm here. Jookie's thrown a shoe. I did exercise the bay."

"Leave Jookie for the day, then."

"I planned to, until he gets the shoe replaced. I came up for lunch."

Amanda put her glasses back in place and retrieved the

ribbon, tying back her hair as she turned her back on the two males and looked out of the window.

Her eyes were blind to the view, however. She was embarrassed to be caught in such circumstances. She should never have been such a willing participant.

She could still feel Mac's kisses, her breath coming more quickly at the remembrances. She hadn't felt like this before.

How funny John-Michael must view them. His Dad and the new neighbor. She smiled a little. High drama it was not. Living on a ranch, he wouldn't be unaware of the physical aspects. For a moment, Amanda wished she was unaware of them. Mac was too attractive. She took a deep breath.

"Here you go."

Turning, she saw Mac standing several feet away, check extended.

Suppressing a smile, she reached for it, scanned it. One hundred dollars.

"Thank you." She risked a quick look to his face; it was closed. "I'll remind you, I don't plan to sell any time soon."

"I know. Maybe you'll change your mind."

"I'll come for a lesson today or tomorrow, if it's all right," John-Michael said.

"Fine. Whenever. I'll be home or at the creek."

She folded the check and stuffed it into her jeans" pocket.

"Do you want a ride home?" Mac asked, still standing several feet away.

It was tempting.

"No, it's a nice walk. Downhill, too, this time."

"See you later, Mandy," John-Michael said.

"Bye, John-Michael, Mac." She left, head held high.

It was Sunday afternoon before John-Michael appeared. Amanda heard the horse and went to greet him when he arrived.

"Hi."

"Hi. I hope it's a convenient time for a lesson," he asked.

"This is a good time."

Joining her on the deck, he seemed more unsure of himself than before.

"Before we start, I'm sorry if I was out of line teasing the other day. Dad yelled at me after you left. I didn't mean to be insulting," John- Michael said, fingering his guitar awkwardly.

"No problem. Your dad over-reacted. He shouldn't have said anything. I knew you were teasing."

"He's been like a bear with a sore paw lately. Worse than before." He gave her a sly look. "You wouldn't like to come up and charm him out of it, would you?"

"Watch it, John-Michael or no more lessons. I irritate your father as much as you say you do, if not lots more."

"Didn't seem like it the other day."

"John-Michael!"

"Okay, I get it. I've practiced while you were gone. See if I've improved."

He sat down on one of the frayed deck chairs, put his

guitar in place and began playing. Amanda could see a definite improvement. It was heartening for a teacher to have such an apt pupil.

"You're doing very well." She spoke warmly when he had finished. "Let's continue."

She taught him more chords, new timing and wrote out several new songs to practice. She showed him how to read music, though what they'd practiced so far had been from familiarity.

When he was leaving, John-Michael paused.

"You ride, don't you?"

"Sure do."

"Want to go on a picnic tomorrow with me? I know a nice field where we can eat. It has a nice view. I thought a way to say thank you for all you're teaching me."

"I'm a sucker for nice views and good companionship. I'd like to go. Shall I come late morning?"

"Yes or I can bring a horse here."

"I'll walk up and meet you there. What shall I bring?"

"Nothing. I'll fix the lunch. Thank you for the lesson. Thanks for all the lessons."

"You're welcome, John-Michael. I'll see you tomorrow."

She waved to him as he rode away, his words from earlier echoing in her head. So Mac was in a bad temper, was he? Disappointed at the interruption? Amanda frowned. If he were, why not come to see her? He certainly knew where she lived.

Maybe John-Michael was exaggerating, or maybe Mac was only upset at being caught kissing Timber's newest layabout. She ought to get that cleared up. But how?

Just come out and say, I'm not a some unemployed ne'er do well. I'm a country singer and make tons of money and am known all over the country?

Hardly. She'd wait until it came up casually in conversation.

Nine

John-Michael, bulging saddle-bags slung over one shoulder, led the way from the big house to the barn the next morning when Amanda arrived. The barn was large, with lofts towering above the stalls, hay from last winter still remaining. When the summer's crop was in, the loft would again be filled to its rafters with enough hay for feed all winter.

"Jessie's a good one."

John-Michael stopped beside a stall, looking over the rail at the brown mare gravely staring back. One white streak blazed down her face.

"I'll saddle her for you."

Amanda took a deep breath, savoring the mingled scents of hay, horse and manure. It brought back a hundred-and-one memories. She'd grown up on a ranch in Colorado. Her parents still ran the place. While cattle was their main focus, one couldn't ranch without horses. She'd spent half her life on the back of a horse.

"I can manage, if you show me the tack."

She'd ridden since she was five.

"Sure. Here's a halter. We'll take them to the post near

the tack room, less distance to carry all the gear."

"A man after my own heart," Amanda said easily. "Lead on."

She competently put the halter on the docile mare, snapped on a lead line and opened the stall.

John-Michael brought out his chestnut and led him to the opposite end of the barn from where they had entered. Amanda followed, through the large opening, then to the left.

Immediately adjacent to the barn was the tack room, a hitching rail before it. Tethering the horses, John-Michael showed Amanda where the tack was. In only minutes, both were busy saddling the horses.

"Oh, oh," John-Michael said softly. "Here comes trouble."

"What?" Amanda looked up as Mac rode into the yard, stopping behind the chestnut gelding, regarding them.

"Hi, Dad," John-Michael said.

Mac nodded, his eyes on Amanda.

She licked her lips, conscious of his regard, and continued her activity, feeling suddenly awkward and clumsy.

"Going riding?" Mac asked.

"Yes. Thought I'd show Mandy around. Have a picnic up near the point."

"I see."

Mac continued to watch them. The silence stretched out endlessly.

Amanda finished first, but was in no hurry to draw attention to the fact. Before John-Michael was ready, however, Mac spoke again.

"Mind if I join you?"

John-Michael looked up in surprise, then pleasure filled his face.

"Sure Dad, glad to have you." He paused. "I guess we have enough food for three."

"I won't eat much," Mac promised, his gaze still on Amanda.

"Oh, I'm sure there's plenty."

John-Michael was ready. He led his horse away from the rail and mounted. Mac remained where he was, watching Amanda.

"Need any help?" he asked. "You mount from the left."

She threw him a scathing look. "I know."

Leading her horse a few steps from the rail, she double checked the cinch and mounted. It had been a year or more since she'd been on a horse--at her last visit home to Colorado. But one never forgot.

She loved riding, and wondered suddenly why she hadn't done much of it in the last few years. The pressures of work were not so demanding she couldn't have spared some time for riding. Not that circling in some prissy arena would be the same as riding the range.

"Oh, yes. You're a ranch gal, I forgot. That cowboy hat you wear should remind me," Mac murmured, drawing up beside her as they left the barn yard and began descending along a trail that skirted one of the pastures. John-Michael was in the lead.

"I was raised on a cattle ranch in Colorado."

"Gave it up for the carefree work free life in San Francisco, eh? Ranching's hard work."

"I'm not against hard work--" she began. Was now the time to tell him what she did, why she had taken her trip?

He interrupted and the moment was gone.

"As long as it's someone else and you can sit around and make beautiful music."

"Some people like music," she snapped.

"Sure, but for entertainment and relaxation once their tasks for the day is finished."

"Someone has to make music for other people to enjoy."

"Hey, you two, come on."

John-Michael was a dozen yards or more ahead, turned in his saddle.

"I thought you wanted to see the place, Mandy, not fight with Dad."

Amanda urged her horse forward, catching up.

"Yes, I do. Sorry, but your father drives me nuts." She shook her head.

"We mustn't offend our guest's gentle sensibilities," Mac said joining them. "From now on, I'll be the model host and guide. Please note on your left is a five acre pasture. It will support over ten head of horses during our growing season, with supplements. We have irrigation for continuous growth of grass during the summer months. Ahead is another pasture."

The tour of the ranch was thorough and informative, though once or twice Amanda suspected Mac was deliberately throwing facts and figures furiously at her to try to overwhelm her.

She listened intently, concentrating on keeping it all straight, in spite of him. She couldn't be expected to remember all the statistics. The basics of ranching she already knew well.

John-Michael led the way when the trail began to narrow. Amanda followed with Mac bringing up the rear. Curving through the trees, switching back as the terrain grew steeper, the trail cut through the undergrowth. In some places, the branches and leaves met across their path, the horses forcing them apart as they continued their plodding climb.

The air was cool in the dappled shade, a small breeze ruffling the uppermost limbs of the tall evergreens. Birds fluttered, squirrels chattered and mysterious rustling in the undergrowth could be heard now that conversation was impossible.

Amanda's heart swelled with happiness. She loved this land, she loved riding. Maybe she could get a horse, if she could arrange her travel schedule to warrant enough usage to justify the expense. Maybe she could even work out some arrangement with Mac for boarding the horse.

She stifled a laugh at that. She could imagine how co-operative he'd be to make her life more appealing in Timber when all he wanted was for her to leave so he could obtain her land.

No, she'd have to find another solution.

"We're here," John-Michael called.

The riders burst forth from the trees into the bright, sunlit open field, surrounded on three sides by the thick

Sierra forest. On the fourth side the meadow ended in a slope down, giving way to sky and endless mountains and valleys to the south of the field.

"Oh!"

Amanda's eyes lit up with the sight. It was magnificent. Involuntarily she stopped her horse, gazing at the smoky mounds in the distance. In one valley a glint of light suggested a river or lake.

John-Michael dismounted, tethering his horse. Mac followed suit, looking to Amanda, still enthralled with the view.

"Need help?" he asked, reaching up to grasp her by the waist.

"I can manage," she protested, as the warmth of his fingers penetrated her shirt.

It seemed effortless, the ease with which he lifted her from the saddle and set her down on the grass.

Amanda felt her heart race. She kept her eyes fixed on his throat, the brown column rising from his blue-checked shirt, the pulse at the base strong and steady.

"Thanks."

She didn't recognize the thready voice as her own. She took a deep breath to strengthen it. Stepping back, she was reluctant to break contact, still was realistic enough to realize safety lay in distance.

"You're welcome."

A trace of amusement sounded.

"Can I help unpack?"

Amanda joined John-Michael. He'd already pulled his saddle-bags from his horse and was moving towards a flat area nearby.

145

"We can pull everything out and start eating."

Amanda settled herself on the warm grass, the forest behind her, the view in front of her. Contentedly, she sat in the blazing sun, munching on a sandwich as she gazed off into the distance, not talking, only half listening as John-Michael and Mac exchanged remarks.

Replete from eating, Amanda's eyes began to grow heavier, the balmy air and hot sun joining to make her positively sleepy. Slowly she sank back upon the scented grass, pulling her hat over her eyes, her lids closing. The warmth of the sun was like a gentle blanket, the breeze moving softly against her skin, keeping her from getting too hot.

Amanda drifted off to sleep.

"But Dad, there's got to be some time when it's okay. What about secret agents? You don't think they can function without deceit."

Gradually Amanda was becoming aware of the man and boy talking. Bit by bit she became more awake. She remained lying down, idly listening, not at first understanding the trend of the conversation, still dozing.

Mac hadn't replied immediately to John-Michael's comment. When he did, Amanda had almost forgotten what John-Michael said.

"Probably most of our problems in the world today are due to deceit of one form or another. But, I grant you, due to the way things are, it might be necessary for a spy or whatever you want to call him to be deceitful. But that doesn't apply to day-to-day living, especially here in Timber. Deception is wrong, John-Michael, it is not a basis for any kind of interaction."

"I still think it is acceptable in some circumstances," he muttered.

"Like what?" he asked sharply.

"I don't know. Like if you really didn't like a lady's dress and she asks you, so you say it is pretty or something."

"That's hardly the same thing, though a really clever person can come up with an honest reply which won't insult or hurt the lady. I know I'm rather rigid in my views on this, but there it is. A person's either straightforward or not. Ones that aren't, can't be trusted. Better to stay away from them. I have very little tolerance for lies and deception."

"Me, too, Dad. Only sometimes it might be justified. That's all I'm trying to say."

"Um." Mac's reply was non-committal.

"Billy Oldmyer's folks are having a big barbecue next weekend. I think most of the guys from school are going. It's a good chance to see everyone again if I can go. It seems like a long time since school got out." John-Michael changed the subject.

Amanda lost track of the conversation, caught up in Mac's words on lies and deceit, wondering what had been the starting point of the conversation. Why they were discussing deceit in the first place?

What would he think when he discovered his view of her was based on a lie by omission? She wanted to share with him her reasons for not letting people know who she was, but now wondered if she dare reveal it and still maintain some sort of friendly relationship. He seemed so very adamant against deceit of any sort.

On the other hand, she couldn't envisage herself adhering to this role he assigned her for years ahead.

Once she was comfortable around her neighbors, and they accepted her for herself, she had no objection to the whole world knowing what she did for a living. She was proud of her work, of her accomplishments. It was just initially that she didn't want those accomplishments to affect her acceptance in the community.

What a quandary. She wanted Mac to think well of her. Why, she refused to closely examine. If she wanted to clear it up, she had better do it soon. Before it got worse.

With the decision made, she stretched, coming fully awake and slowly sat up.

"Gosh, Sleepyhead, we thought you'd sleep all afternoon," John-Michael said.

"Your snoring scared all the animals off," Mac said.

"I don't snore," she replied disdainfully.

"How do you know?" John-Michael asked.

"Someone must have told her," Mac replied, his eyes watching her.

She gave him a very speaking glance, unaware it had no effect because her sunglasses hid her face. "Someone did, as a matter of fact," she said sweetly, "my sister."

"I didn't know you had a sister," John-Michael said with interest.

"Oh, yes. I'm one of five, two girls and three boys. Plus, my mother's from a large family, my dad's from a large family and their brothers and sisters also married people from big families. I had forty-three cousins within a ten mile radius of the town I grew up in."

"Gosh, I'm an only child; Dad is too. I don't know about my mother."

"She had a sister, but no kids, last I heard," Mac said, gathering up the remnants of lunch. "I've work to do. Are you two heading back now?"

"Yes. I've some things to do, too. It's been lovely, though. Thanks for asking me, John-Michael. You have a beautiful place here."

"I'm glad you like it, Mandy. Come and ride any time. That's all right with you, isn't it Dad?"

Mac was quiet for a moment and Amanda couldn't resist, "Thinking up an honest answer that won't insult me, Mac?"

"Eavesdropping, were you?"

She grinned easily.

"Only the last few minutes, just as I was waking. Don't worry. I won't come riding if I'm not wanted," she said with scarcely any pang.

"I'll go with you a few times, make sure you can find your way around--and don't neglect or abuse my horses."

"Charming." She stood, reconsidered. "Thank you, I might like it after all."

The two of them, alone, riding--what better opportunity for sharing confidences?

Mac left them before they reached the barn, riding across the field, at ease in the saddle, his hat low on his face to protect it from the sun.

Amanda watched until he was lost from view. It'd been a nice day, made even more so by Mac's unexpected arrival.

John-Michael was waiting for her when she turned back.

"Tell me about growing up with forty-three cousins. It must have been fun."

"Oh, it was. We're all close, some of each age, you know, so everyone has someone special. Holidays are the best. Aunt Meg has the biggest place, so we almost always go there for Christmas."

Amanda recounted holidays on the ride to the barn. John-Michael listened with great interest, asking questions, laughing, sharing her memories wistfully.

"Why did you ever leave?" he asked as they unsaddled the horses.

"Well, a bunch of us work together so we try to get home a few times each year, though it's been a while since we've been back this last stretch."

She knew she'd be home for Thanksgiving, but suddenly that seemed a long way off.

"Everyone's all grown, too. Some married and moved away. We still see each other whenever we can. It was great fun growing up and I loved it. But I like California, too. This is where I want my home, for my kids to have happy memories."

"Yeah, I guess so." John-Michael was quiet as he brushed down his mount, led him to the corral and turned him loose inside. Amanda was right behind him.

As they watched the horses amble away, he spoke again, pensively.

"I guess if Dad and Mom had stayed together, there'd have been more kids. It's hard to imagine, though."

"Your father's still fairly young. He could marry again,

have more."

"It wouldn't be the same. I'm almost grown now. Well, maybe I wouldn't have liked sharing anyway. Want to come to the house for a Coke?"

"No, thank you, some other time if I may. I've had fun today. Thank you for asking me. It's a great ranch, John-Michael. I'd like to come again."

"Sure, any time. I might come tomorrow for another lesson."

"Good. See you then." With a smile and wave, she was off.

She couldn't help wishing Mac had ridden back to the barn with them. That he'd been the one to offer her free access to his ranch.

Ten

Amanda dressed with great care for Elizabeth Burke's dinner party. She hadn't seen Mac since the picnic. John-Michael had come for another lesson, not referring to the picnic, nor to the embrace he'd interrupted, but smiling at Amanda more than before.

She, of course, didn't refer to either. What could she say? It had only been a kiss. Only a kiss? She grew warm all over whenever she thought about it. Well, then, maybe a little more than merely a kiss.

Amanda decided to throw caution to the wind and really dress for dinner. If someone recognized her, so be it. Her reason for keeping her identity secret now seemed silly. She made no effort to make friends in town. She kept to herself and soaked up the solitude. Time to be herself and let the chips fall where they may.

She wanted to look her best. She washed and curled her hair, brushing it until it gleamed, soft and wavy around her face. Make-up was subtly donned, enhancing her blue eyes and high cheek bones. She wanted to look especially nice–for the other guests, she told herself, thinking of a particular other guest. Her intent was to forever erase the hippie image, if she could.

Her dress was a soft, creamy light-weight fabric with high ruffled collar, long sleeves with ruffles capturing her wrists. It clung to her figure, outlining her firm breasts, slender waist and rounded hips. Amanda was pleased to see she had put on a little weight since her summer began. She'd been too thin at the end of her last tour. This dress made her feel feminine and alluring.

She wrinkled her nose and turned from the mirror.

She was not out to allure anyone.

The dress swayed gently as she walked displaying her figure to advantage as she moved. Mac and John-Michael would be here soon to pick her up. She didn't want to keep them waiting.

Nervously she fingered her skirt, then chided herself for her foolishness. She, who had performed many times before thousands of people, was nervous about a man coming to pick her up to drive her to a small dinner party. Honestly! One would think it mattered.

Gazing out the window, Amanda reflected that it did matter. She wanted him to like her. Maybe more than like her. She wanted it to be for herself, however. For Mac to value her for what she was, not any fame she had achieved.

In a moment's conversation she could clear up the less than complimentary image he held, could clear up any misconceptions about her situation. Let him know she was a hard-working, successful member of society.

Still, stubbornly, Amanda clung to the notion of being wanted for herself, as she was, not for what she'd accomplished. She wanted him to want her as he knew her.

Let the explanations come later.

Sighing softly, she wondered if it were a pipe-dream.

She heard the truck before she saw it turn into the drive. Only it wasn't the old gray truck, but a gleaming maroon and silver sedan with MHR entwined in a fancy monogram on the doors. It looked new, powerful, expensive. Obviously the vehicle they must use when going to shows and rodeos. It reflected the successful ranching endeavor Amanda suspected Mac ran more than his old gray pickup.

Fluffing her hair one last time, she grabbed her handbag. Taking a deep breath, just as she did to calm herself before going on stage, Amanda flung open the door.

Both Mac and John-Michael were getting out of the truck. Both were dressed in dark jeans and snowy white shirts. While appreciating how nice they both looked, Amanda was especially conscious of how superbly Mac filled his out. The lack of his hat was a startling change, his auburn waves gleaming in the late sun. John-Michael remained by the truck as Mac advanced to the steps, studying her, his face impassive.

"Hi." Amanda smiled brightly. "Not your usual vehicle, I see."

"No, this one's for show. Thought it more appropriate for tonight than the gray one. Glad now I did. You look very nice."

His eyes strayed to her lips as he spoke.

Amanda felt the nervousness again, quickly licking her lips. She moved towards the truck, admiring it. Doing her best to keep everything on a casual basis.

"Hi, Mandy," John-Michael easily greeted her. "Don't think we'll be too crowded, do you?"

She slid in as John-Michael held the passenger door. Mac climbed in the driver's side, only inches from Amanda. When John-Michael sat down in the back, Mac started the engine.

As he drove away from the cabin Amanda became more and more aware of Mac's every move. He brushed against her turning to see out of the back window when reversing to the main drive; the contact sent vibrations throughout Amanda's whole body.

Afraid she'd give herself away, she turned to John-Michael.

"Been practicing?"

"Not much, I've been busy. I like your hair that way. It's pretty, all fluffy."

"Thanks."

Amanda looked out of the windshield.

John- Michael had been her major concern. He was the only one she knew for certain listened to her music, had at least an some downloads.

If he didn't recognize her, perhaps she exaggerated her fame. Imperceptibly, she relaxed.

It was, fortunately, not a long drive.

Elizabeth Burke's house was as stately as its owner. The old Victorian residence, freshly painted, sat in the middle of a manicured lawn, with formal flower-beds flanking the path. A small fence surrounded the yard. There were already two other vehicles drawn up before it when Mac pulled the truck to the curb.

In only a moment Elizabeth was greeting them at her door ushering them into her living room. Two other couples were already present, an older man and a much younger blonde woman on the sofa. Near the fireplace a man and woman about Mac's age were studying a figurine.

"Mac. So good to see you."

The blonde rose swiftly and came to meet him, smiling prettily. "It's been too long!"

"Sally, may I introduce Mandy Smith," Elizabeth said, intercepting Sally. "Sally Sutherland. And her father, Henry Sutherland. Henry's Timber's pharmacist," Elizabeth said.

Mr. Sutherland had risen and followed his daughter to greet the newcomers, though at a more leisurely pace.

"How do you?" Amanda murmured, shaking hands.

The couple by the fireplace turned, friendly smiles of welcome on their faces as they joined the others.

"Ron and Pamela Haversham. This is Mandy Smith, she's a neighbor of Mac's. The singer I was telling you about."

"How do you do?" Amanda murmured again, smiling at the Havershams.

"Ron's on the Festival Committee, so you'll see quite a bit of him as the time draws nearer," Pamela said with a fond look at her husband. "Have you sung in front of a large audience before?"

"Yes," Amanda answered briefly.

"You might even find a career in it," Mac murmured softly, for her ears alone.

Amanda refused to rise to the bait. She smiled up at him. "Maybe."

Sally placed a perfectly manicured hand on Mac's arm. "Come and talk to me. I know you aren't the least interested in the festival."

Amanda glanced at Sally, then back at Mac, a mischievous smile lighting her face. There was a woman on the make if she ever saw one.

"Yes, do go talk with your friend. I'll be fine with my new acquaintances."

With a hard look at Amanda, as if warning her to watch herself, he went with Sally. They sat on the sofa, Sally plunging immediately into an animated discussion designed to absorb Mac's full attention.

The others remained where they were.

"Elizabeth said you're a neighbor of Mac's. Are you the one who bought Cora's place?" Henry Sutherland asked.

"Yes. I have lots to do with it before it'll be the way I envisage it. But I'm very excited about the potential. It's the first home I've bought, you know," she confided.

"Where are you from?" Pamela asked.

"Most recently, L.A."

"That explains it," Ron said. "Anything would be better than L.A., even a cabin that needs a ton of work done to it."

"Ron, lots of people like L.A," Pamela scolded.

"But not Miss Smith or she'd not be here."

"Right you are. I already love Timber. But, please, call me Mandy."

"Glad to. I'm Ron."

"Henry."

"Pamela."

"I'm John-Michael. Is this a new game Aunt Elizabeth thought up?"

John-Michael joined the group, coming up easily and standing near Amanda.

"No, dear. We are just introducing ourselves again," Elizabeth said. "Would you help serve the cocktails? I seem to have lost your father."

John-Michael glanced at the sofa smiling at Sally when she waved to him.

"Yes, I guess you did. Sure, I'll help."

John-Michael took the orders and efficiently matched drinks to the proper individuals. Sally and Mac remained isolated from the others, who moved as a group to sit on the chairs and ottoman between the stone fireplace and long windows overlooking the side garden.

Even though they sat apart, Amanda was soon aware of Mac's eyes on her. Twice she looked up, her gaze locking with his, driving all thoughts from her head. Causing her to lose the thread of the conversation around her.

After the second incident, she vowed to refrain from looking in his direction, though she was still conscious of his regard, his constant surveillance. It was almost a physical strain to keep her gaze within the group, to refrain from looking at Mac.

"Do you have a job up here?" Pamela asked. "Are you working?"

"Not right now. I'm sort of taking the summer off," Amanda replied.

"Are you a teacher?" Henry inquired.

"She's teaching me guitar," John-Michael volunteered

from his perch on the arm of Amanda's chair.

"Wonderful. A good accomplishment to have," Ron said. "I think it's good to have a musical outlet if you have even a spec of talent."

"I often wished I did. We enjoy sitting around in the evenings on the patio and listening to quiet melodies played in the background. Not your type of music, young man, but I'm sure what you play will give you many hours of pleasure, John-Michael," Pamela said.

"Wait until you hear Mandy sing. You'll love it. Talk about listening pleasure," John-Michael said, smiling down at her, his eyes holding hers. "Everyone who hears her loves her. She's very popular."

Amanda's eyes widened. *He knows who I am!* she thought, startled.

Then amused.

He'd never said anything.

As she looked questioningly at him, he smiled and nodded slightly. She smiled back at him, closing her right eye in a quick wink.

At least I think he likes me for myself and not for who I am. I wonder how long he's known, she mused, turning back to the others. She'd find out later.

Amanda was surprised to learn when dinner was announced, that Elizabeth had a cook. Somehow the rugged independence of the rural community hadn't prepared her for the trappings of the city. Yet, upon closer observation, the cook had probably been with Elizabeth for years; she looked to be the same age. A fitting accompaniment to the stately elegance of the old Victorian house.

159

The party moved to the formal dining room. A large mahogany table beneath a crystal chandelier dominated the room. It was formally set with fine china, crystal and silver. Mac sat at the head, with Sally and Amanda on either side. Elizabeth was opposite him, with Henry and Ron on her left and right. John- Michael sat opposite Pamela, who was between her husband and Amanda.

The meal was quickly served--soup first, then salad and the entree, fresh mountain trout in a tasty, tangy sauce. The food was delicious.

Conversation lagged while the guests began their meal, the silence a tribute to the excellent cuisine. As the dinner progressed, Amanda was entertained by Sally's rather obvious attempts to monopolize Mac.

Observing more than participating, Amanda deduced Sally'd love nothing more than to be the next Mrs. John MacKensie.

From Mac's scowling expression, Amanda didn't give Sally much of a chance.

Elizabeth's voice broke into the small silence after an amusing story Sally told, swinging Amanda's attention to that end of the table.

"... of course, in my younger day, a woman stayed home and tended the household."

"And so they still should." Sally jumped in. " I think being a homemaker is a full-time career in itself. Every woman should strive for that."

Sally's eyes slid quickly to Mac, quickly away again.

Elizabeth nodded. "I agree."

"If they can and want," Amanda couldn't resist inserting.

"Huh?" Sally said, rather inelegantly.

"If a woman wants to be a homemaker, fine. It's not always feasible, either economically or emotionally these days," Amanda said.

Seven pairs of eyes stared at her. Open mouth, insert foot, she thought wryly, glancing around the table.

"Well, yes, I can see if someone had to work because of money," Sally reluctantly concurred, "but, otherwise, I can't understand a woman wanting to go out everyday to a job, competing with men. Her place is in her husband's home, providing for him."

Amanda wrinkled her nose.

"If I ever get married, I'd expect my husband to give me the same respect and support I'd give him. A career that was important to me would, by that mutual respect, also be important to my husband."

"If you want to work, don't get married," Sally said.

"Men aren't given that advice," Amanda said. "They can have a career and a home life. Why can't a woman do that, too?"

"I still say a wife's place is in her husband's home. What do you think, Mac?"

"I'm old-fashioned enough to agree. I think it's a fine profession for a woman, taking care of a home, a husband, a family."

Sally beamed around the table. Mac sided with her.

"Perhaps being at home all the time isn't enough for some people. Look at my mother," John-Michael interrupted. "Maybe if she'd had something else to do, she wouldn't have run off. I think she was bored."

From the stunned silence around the table, Amanda realized the taboo he'd broken. Her anger flared. The poor boy. He probably missed his mother, but because of the coddling everyone did to appease Mac, he was unable to talk about her, to resolve any feelings he had, get clarification of what really happened.

"Maybe," Amanda replied as the others remained awkwardly silent, "but she was a fool to leave you behind, sweetie."

John-Michael shot her a grateful glance, then looked apprehensively at his father. Mac's face was closed, his eyes narrowed, going from Amanda to John-Michael and back to Amanda.

Sally reached out a consoling hand.

"Maybe she was bored," Amanda spoke up. "There isn't much to do keeping a house tidy these days and with neighbors so far away here in the country, maybe she yearned for something more than she got. I know I would."

"Well, I've been a full-time homemaker and worked outside. If you have a job you like, it's rewarding to feel a part of the community. I enjoyed it when I was home all the time, but I had small children that needed me. Once they were older, it was boring to stay home all day alone, no friends close by." Pam spoke. "With all the modern appliances we enjoy, the actual work involved in keeping a house is greatly reduced. I like working now. It's not so bad, do you think, Ron?"

"No. I'm happy you're happy, Pamela."

Amanda smiled at them. Was this another couple like Dave and Evie?

"I still think a wife's place is in the home," Sally said stubbornly.

"And I believe marriage should be a partnership, a sharing of two lives, of whatever the two lives are doing, not the abdication of one in total absorption to the other," Amanda said clearly, meeting and holding Mac's eyes for a long moment, breaking away to look over to Sally.

"Anyway, Sally, it's a useless conversation. I've had these views for years. You probably have had yours for years, too. I know I'm too set to change."

Amanda smiled at the other woman, inviting comment. Almost reluctantly, Sally smiled back.

"You are right, I am too set to change, either."

"Mandy pans for gold." John-Michael changed the subject.

The others, eager to lighten the atmosphere, joined in with questions and advice, with an occasional derisive comment thrown in by Mac. Amanda took it all in good part and the rest of the meal passed smoothly.

Coffee was served in the living room. This time everyone sat together, although Sally stayed as close to Mac as she could. The conversation was general and Amanda enjoyed herself, learning more about her new acquaintances while not revealing more about herself than she wished.

When it was time to leave, Amanda and John-Michael were first to the car, but had to wait for Mac, who walked Sally to her car. As they watched them, John-Michael said,

"Sally'd like to marry Dad, you know."

"Do you like her?" Amanda asked.

She did know, it was quite obvious.

"She's all right. She's been after Dad for years." He was quiet for a moment. "I don't think he'll ever marry her, though. He's never even kissed her."

"You don't know that."

Amanda's face grew warm and she was grateful for the night's cloaking darkness. Mac had kissed her several times. John-Michael only knew of one time. Amanda wouldn't mind if Mac kissed her again. She shook her head—what was she thinking?

"I know," the boy said.

What could she say to that? There was no need. Mac gave a final wave and moved to join them.

Amanda was achingly aware of Mac when he climbed in. His leg was only inches from hers, his arm almost touching her as he drove through the blackness, the headlights the only illumination on this moonless night.

Reaching her cabin, he stopped the truck with the lights illuminating the steps and front door. Amanda drew her key from her handbag before getting out.

"I'll walk you up," Mac said.

John-Michael got out to open her door. "Good night, Mandy," he said, climbing back in the front and turning on the radio while he waited for his father.

"Thank you for taking me."

Amanda reached the front door and unlocked it. Just as the door swung open, the lights of the truck went out, plunging them into total darkness.

"What the--John-Michael!"

Mac turned and roared at his son.

Amanda gave a small giggle. "He's being tactful."

"What does that mean?"

Mac's voice lost some of its anger.

She swallowed.

"Only that John-Michael thought we might be more comfortable saying good night in the dark." Amanda trailed off, realizing where that might lead.

Mac's hand brushed her cheek, found her shoulders and drew her slowly up to him.

"He's smarter than I thought," he said softy, lowering his head to hers.

Amanda thrilled at his touch, reveled in the feel of his fingers as they threaded themselves in her hair, drew themselves through the silken strands. He tilted her head to suit him, thumbs along her jaw bone, as his mouth came down to hers.

His lips were warm and persuasive, drawing a willing response from her as she twined her arms around his neck. His kiss tantalized her, causing sensations she "had known only once before. In his embrace. She lost track of time as the kiss went on and on.

"I want you, Mandy," he said softly against her mouth, his breath mingling with hers.

She felt a small frisson of pleasure course through her.

"John-Michael," she protested.

"I know."

He kissed her again and again, his arms locked around her back, pulling her hard against him. Over and over he rained kisses along her jaw, cheek, back to her mouth. His lips were demanding, his touch filling her senses with a heady passion.

"Not tonight, but soon," he said, in between kisses.

He trailed his lips down her throat, back to her cheek, finding her mouth again.

"You're so beautiful. Do you know what effect that has on a man?"

Amanda could hardly breathe. His body against hers was exciting. She wanted Mac to keep kissing her, to move his hands as he had the other time. For the moment to go on and on. Forget about John-Michael. Forget about everything, save the feelings Mac could bring.

Finally, reluctantly, slowly, he eased his hold, drew back. With one last, brief kiss, only lips touching, he turned and left.

The car reversed and reached the main drive before Mac turned on the headlights, sparing Amanda the harsh glare. She watched the lights disappear through the trees, thoughts churning. Lightly she traced her mouth with her tongue, her lips just slightly swollen from the pressure of his kisses.

A smile lifted the corners of her mouth. What a wonderful end to an evening. And there was promise of... of what?

She had a sudden, dreadful thought. What if Mac thought she went in for casual sex.

Just because he thought her a hippie, did he also think she went in for love-ins and all the other casual relations the old hippie image held?

Eleven

The telephone installer woke Amanda early the next morning. He was a cheery old man who talked steadily as he wired the cabin from a line he strung outside.

Amanda liked him, made him coffee and listened to his tales of various customers and the ingenuity it'd taken for him to connect some of their remote dwellings with the lines from the local telephone company.

Hers, in comparison, was an easy morning's work.

When the man finished and left, Amanda used her new phone to call Dave. After giving him her new number, she continued,

"Do me a favor and check on the status of my furniture. It was so hectic coming back from Nashville and trying to arrange for them to move my stuff up and still get back up here on the day I said I would, I don't have a definite idea of where it is and when it's due to arrive."

"I'll check it out and let you know," he promised. "By the way, I got two new songs from Bob Clive that you might want to listen to. I thought they'd be good for the new album if you like them."

"Sounds promising, what are they like?"

Bob Clive was a songwriter whose music Amanda especially enjoyed performing. He had written several of her most successful songs and she was always eager to try his work when he wrote another one.

"One's a ballad, the other one's fast, like Boatman's Shanty Boy. When can you try them? Shall I send them up to you? Did you take your laptop?"

"No, no internet service up here. Though maybe I can get now that I have a phone. I'll have to see. But in the meantime, just mail them. Give me a few days to check them out and I'll call you. I've written another one, too. I don't know how you'll like it, though."

Actually she believed Dave would like the song Dave but probably not the sentiment behind it.

"Why wouldn't I like it? I like all your songs. I talked to the others about your rural festival on Labor Day. We'll be up in Timber the morning of the event, full gear and all. It's a noon show, right?"

"Actually I think Miss Burke said we'd go on at two o'clock. Close enough, I guess. You should be here by late morning so we can set up. We can have a picnic, too. How's Evie?"

"Big as a house. She won't make the picnic. I'll let you know when I'm a daddy. Thanks for the number. I'll call you about the furniture as soon as I find out."

"Thanks. Hi to all."

Amanda hung up slowly. A phone was certainly an added asset to her cabin. Now she'd have the best of both words, rural living, yet instant contact with whoever she wanted to talk to regarding business. Perhaps she could

168

work it so plans and transactions could be handled, at least initially, by phone. And if she got wifi, the opportunities would become limitless.

Wandering out to the deck, she drew up a chair, tilted back, feet on the railing. She could imagine conducting business from her deck. What a set up.

Gazing out at the trees, she thought of what she and Dave discussed. She had a new song, but was wondering how he'd take the message it gave.

Idly, she hummed it through, then again. It was good. She went to get paper, pencil and her guitar. The music had been in her head all summer, the words gradually growing as the days passed. She hummed it again, strumming the guitar.

Time drifted by as she worked on the lyrics, the tempo. It was almost finished, but she wanted it to be perfect before singing it for the band. She wanted to present it at its best.

At one point she thought she heard the motor of the big gray pick-up, but nothing came into view and she grinned ruefully. No more wishful thinking; concentrate on the work at hand.

It grew warmer as the sun reached its zenith. Amanda was clad in the usual jeans and cotton shirt. Her feet were bare and, as she sat with them on the railing, she considered going inside to change. Shorts would be much more appropriate in the hot afternoon. But first, she'd perfect this last section.

Preoccupied with the composition, Amanda failed to hear the truck when it really did approach until it was actually turning into her drive.

Throat dry, heart tripping, she stood up, placing her music face down on the table. It might be John- Michael, he drove the truck sometimes.

A smile lit her face, however, as Mac climbed out and strode to the deck.

Amanda moved to meet him. "Hi, what brings you by?"

"Messenger service," he replied, skipping stairs, joining her on the deck, his gaze roaming over her figure, reminding her of the first time they met. His masculine assessment didn't annoy her this time, quite the contrary; she was warmed and excited by it.

"Aunt Elizabeth's having a group meeting next week regarding the festival. She wants you to come if you can. I don't know why she didn't let you know last night, unless they just decided this morning. Anyway, she asked me to come by and let you know."

"When is it?"

"Next Tuesday, about ten."

"If I can get there," she said diffidently. "Are you going? May I get a lift from you to your aunt's next Tuesday?" she asked sweetly, looking up at the narrowed, gleaming green eyes.

He was so attractive. Did he have any idea of the feelings his mere presence brought up in her? She moved just a little closer, smiling up to him, flirting.

"Yeah I'm going. I'll give you a ride."

He watched her as she drew near, a small glint of amusement showing.

"It's hot out here, care for some lemonade? I have some made."

"Sounds good."

Amanda entered the cabin, Mac following her inside, closing the door to the day's heat. She looked back, caught in his gaze.

Sweeping his hat off, he tossed it on to the table. Extending one arm, he stopped her move to the kitchen and turned her around to face him. Amanda remembered what he'd said last night. Suddenly she felt butterflies in her stomach. She watched him waiting for his next move.

"Mandy," he said huskily, pulling her close.

"Yes?" she whispered as he lowered his head to give her another kiss.

Amanda felt a sudden surge of pleasure. She reached up to encircle his neck with her arms, threading her fingers through his thick, wavy hair. It was crisp and smooth as her fingers buried themselves in it. Mac's lips were firm and warm, moving against hers.

One hand slipping beneath the back of her loose-fitting shirt, his fingers warm against her soft smooth skin. As he explored her back, she shivered with delight and anticipation, a strong feeling of desire growing within her with the feather light caresses he made against her skin with his hand, his other hand holding her head firmly for his kisses.

She reveled in them, responded to his kisses, scarcely aware of anything but Mac's mouth on hers and his hands on her body.

He raised his head and glanced around. "Why don't

you have a sofa like everyone else, so we could sit down?" he growled, his voice low.

"Cushions are fine."

Amanda led him over, trailing her hands down his arms as she lowered herself to one of the large soft cushions near the wall. Mac sank down beside her and drew her into his arms. His touch was thrilling, exciting. On and on the kiss went, slowly warming Amanda, slowly awakening vague desires and longings.

"Oh, Mandy, girl. You're so soft and pretty," Mac whispered against her ear as his mouth feathered kisses along her cheek, to her throat, down her neck.

She smiled dreamily at his words, eager for his mouth to return to hers.

The shrill, strident ring of the telephone shattered the afternoon stillness.

"What's that? Some kind of alarm?" Mac growled, startled. He pulled away abruptly.

"My phone. I just got it today." She sat up. "I guess I should answer it."

"Yes, I guess you should. Did you have to get the model with the loudest ring?"

Amanda smiled and lithely rose, moving quickly into the kitchen. The ring was harsh in the drowsy afternoon. Could she adjust the loudness?

"Hello?"

"Hi, Mandy, Dave here."

"Hi."

"Your furniture left a few days ago. Should arrive in Timber later this week. They have your address and directions, but don't know you have a phone, so don't wander off or they might dump everything in the front yard."

"I'll stay close. Thanks for checking for me, Dave."

"No problem. I'll talk to you soon."

Amanda replaced the receiver and turned, eager to rejoin Mac. He stood in the doorway, an inscrutable expression on his face.

Gone was the tender look she had seen in his eyes only moments ago.

"Someone's coming," he said, looking out the open door.

Amanda's eyes widened. She could hear the gravel in the driveway. Who was it? John- Michael? She moved to see. Mac remained squarely in the doorway, blocking her way.

"Another time, hmm, Mandy?" he said gently, reaching down to lightly brush against her lips.

"I hope so," she said frankly, giving a small smile. It had been a heady time.

Still the phone had been a lifesaver if she was really having another visitor now.

The sedan stopped and Elizabeth Burke got out of the car.

"Good afternoon, Mandy. How are you?" she called, seeing her in the doorway.

"Hi, Mac. I didn't know you'd be here, too."

"Aunt Elizabeth. Did you worry I wouldn't pass on your invitation?"

"Don't be silly, dear boy."

Amanda hid a smile, darting a quick glance at the "dear boy". A less likely looking boy Amanda couldn't imagine.

"No, I decided to discuss part of the program for the festival with Mandy prior to the meeting."

"That's my cue to leave, then. I'll see you Mandy. Tuesday, if not before."

"Thank you. And ... thanks for stopping by today."

"My pleasure."

She licked her lips as he passed to leave, disappointment flooding through her. It had been wonderful; she was sorry he was leaving.

Elizabeth Burke sat primly on one of the dining chairs after her nephew left.

"I wanted to get this cleared up, my dear. I hope I'm not coming at an inopportune time."

"Not at all. Would you like some lemonade?"

She remembered asking Mac the same thing only a short time ago.

"Not today, thank you, Now, did your group agree to come, too, to sing in the festival?"

"Yes, they'll arrive that morning. I think I heard you say the entertainment wouldn't start until after noon. Is that right?"

"Yes, around two usually. That gives everyone time to eat and be finished so they can then devote full attention to the performance. After the show, there're games, then a huge barbecue and we finish with fireworks after dark. A local high school group will play music at dusk for those who want to dance. We make do for that, but always try for a more professional group for the main feature. I do hope

174

you'll be able to handle it."

Elizabeth frowned and added fretfully, "I do wish Mac'd come. Or at least permit John-Michael to attend. They both miss such good events each year." She shook her head. "Well it can't be helped. Now, we need about an hour's entertainment. Is that too long?"

Amanda smiled. "No problem. We've played large audiences before and usually do fine. I sing country songs, did you know that?"

"Oh, my dear, that will be splendid! That's so very popular in Timber. The rock music doesn't seem too much in demand these days, except for some of the teenagers. Now, if you need anything, loudspeakers or whatever, do make a list for the committee. We'll do our best to get what you need."

Briefly Amanda thought of their traveling bus loaded with a dozen or more costume changes and thousands of dollars' worth of electrical equipment.

"We have all we need," she replied. "We'll just need access to a power source."

"Of course. A large audience won't worry you?" Miss Burke looked concerned.

"No, we've played before large groups before."

Audiences larger than the entire population of Timber.

Elizabeth nodded, satisfied. "Well, I guess that covers it. If you want to set up your equipment early, the stage should be set up by ten or so. It's portable, you know/ We erect it each year for the festival."

She rose. "I look forward to our meeting on Tuesday. You'll have a chance to meet the others working on the committee and we'll get an overview of the entire set of activities so we can see how the day will go."

"I look forward to it, too. I'll see you next week."

As Elizabeth backed her car out, Amanda again marveled at the way the entertainment was handled for such an important event in the little town's social calendar.

No audition, no contract, just a fond great-aunt's acceptance of a high-school boy's evaluation of a new neighbor. How did they know she really could sing? That she was any good? That she could be counted on?

It certainly was a different way of handling a gig than most she experienced.

Turning from the door when Miss Burke left, Amanda's eyes alighted on the cushions, now stacked neatly against the wall. How far would things have gone had the phone not rung and Elizabeth not come by?

Amanda questioned if she'd have drawn back or not? She hugged herself with loneliness, wishing Mac were still here. It seemed a long time until Tuesday.

Mac sounded the horn Tuesday morning. It wasn't necessary. Amanda had been watching for him for over half an hour. She opened her door even as the horn still echoed, running lightly down the shallow stairs and climbing into the truck. Her hair was again pulled back, the tinted glasses in place. Her jeans were new and still dark blue, the cotton top informal but not too casual.

"Good morning," she said brightly. She gave him a warm smile, not letting the disappointment she'd felt the last few days show. She hadn't seen nor spoken to Mac since he left after Elizabeth's unexpected arrival. She'd waited each day, but nothing from Mac MacKensie. He knew she had a phone, but no calls.

"Morning," he replied, setting the truck in motion. He didn't speak again and the ride continued in silence. Mac finally broke it only when Elizabeth's home came into view.

"I'll pick you up in a couple of hours. That should be enough time."

"I thought you were coming to the meeting."

"No, I don't have anything to do with the festival."

"Okay then. Thanks for the ride."

Amanda got out as soon as he had stopped the truck slamming the door and going to the house without a backward glance. Blow hot, blow cold. What made the man tick? She was upset he continued to be so difficult to get to know.

And she wanted to so much.

Elizabeth Burke had the meeting well organized. All points she wanted covered were listed out on agendas she gave everyone. She was firm in keeping the discussion focused on one point at a time.

The concessions committee reported its area under control, with plenty of Cokes, beer, hot dogs, hamburgers and chips being brought in for the townsfolk who didn't want to bring their own food to the festivities.

Ron Haversham was in charge of games. He reported them well in hand--horseshoe setups would be ready by ten. Volley-ball nets set up then as well. Softball was scheduled for after the singing event.

Amanda reported that she had a back-up band that'd be coming for the festival and would be
bringing their own equipment. She gave a list of songs she thought she'd sing, leaving several slots open to be filled that day with songs that were her special trademark.

No sense, if they didn't require it, in letting them all know who she was. Time enough later. But she felt more confident now and, if the exposure came early, it wouldn't matter so much.

There was mild curiosity about the band but when the crafts committee reported, the interest faded. A large number of townspeople were bringing handicrafts to sell at the festival and booths would be set up early to catch the first arrivals.

Elizabeth distributed a list of participants, schedule of events and contact phone numbers. Everyone dutifully added Amanda's number when she informed them she now had a phone.

"The festival should be a resounding success this year and we can all be proud of our contributions." Elizabeth closed the meeting. "I'll be in touch with each of you as the need arises, but see no need for another joint meeting."

Amanda looked for a clock. They'd been less than the two hours Mac estimated. Not that it mattered--she could easily wait out front, it was a pleasant day. When she left with the rest of the committee, however, she was surprised to see the gray truck parked across the road, in the shade.

Though her heart gave a spurt of delight to see him, Amanda tried to school her features to remain as impassive as Mac's.

178

With a small shock, Amanda realized she was growing to love this bitter, disapproving man. She wanted to spend time with him. Bring some happiness if he'd let her. To share her time with him. With a rush of affection, she saw he was watching her cross the road, his eyes following her, his manner and actions speaking louder than his words ever had. She smiled as she climbed into the pick-up.

"Meeting done?" he asked, starting the engine.

"Sure is. The festival plans are in full swing now. It sounds like fun. According to Elizabeth, everyone in town will be there." Amanda looked at him as he kept his eyes on the road. "Are you and John-Michael coming? Can I have a ride?"

Mac shot her a quick look, deep lines of disapproval etched in his face.

"We don't go."

"Why not?" Dangerous ground, she knew. But she wanted them to come. If only for him to know she wasn't the lazy hippie he thought she was.

"We don't go to the festival."

"Well, come this year. I won't always be at them. This may be my only time. You can hear me sing."

Amanda noticed how his hands tightened on the wheel till the knuckles were white. His jaw was clenched, his mouth tight.

She sighed and turned to look out the window. Were the memories still so painful for him? Could he not let the past go? What chance did she ever have against the memory of a runaway wife?

As the driveway drew near, Mac seemed to relax a little.

"Want to come up for lunch?" he asked.

Surprised, Amanda agreed.

"It is so incredibly beautiful up here," she said when they reached Mac's place. "There is a sense of peace and serenity you don't find in many places."

"I know." He looked at her a long moment, then led the way into the house.

"Come into the kitchen." He walked through the living area, Amanda following.

The modern kitchen was surrounded by large windows giving access to the view. The far end of the room was the dining area, with large, sliding glass doors leading to the deck.

Amanda kept silent afraid if she said more about the view he'd think she was gushing.

"Roast beef sandwiches okay?"

Mac was drawing things from the refrigerator.

"Fine." She moved to stand by him, helping a little as they made the sandwiches. Then he took two soft drinks from the refrigerator.

They ate at the table, talking little at first. When hunger had been satisfied, Amanda asked him about the town of Timber, how it came to be, how long his family had been residents. Moving on to other topics, like her life in Colorado.

They skirted some issues, Mac's marriage, Amanda's career. Yet she still felt they were communicating, drawing closer.

Or was it only wishful thinking on her part?

Perhaps one day soon they could trust each other

enough to discuss even the delicate issues they avoided this day.

Amanda realized they were spending the greater part of the afternoon still at the table. He'd made no move to end her visit. Mac probably had work to attend to, but she wasn't going to bring it up and end the pleasant afternoon. It wasn't often they could meet and talk without setting off sparks.

The conversation veered to her cabin, Amanda mentioning that her furniture had arrived and she'd be painting the walls to spruce up the place some more.

"It'll be a big job, though, so I'm putting it off a little," she smiled.

"I had this house repainted a year or so ago. It is a big job, but all places need it every so often."

"Yes, I guess. I haven't seen all of your house. May I?" Amanda asked. The living room she had seen, now the kitchen. She knew John-Michael's bedroom was off the living room, but the rest?

"Sure. This is the kitchen."

Mac rose and led the way back into the living room. Opening John- Michael's door, he stood aside so Amanda could peek into the room. John-Michael had posters over most of the walls: rock stars, the one of the WWE"s Raw champs, one of a bucking bronc at a rodeo. It was remarkably tidy for a teenager's room, she thought.

Down a short hallway Mac opened a door leading to a bathroom. Moving down the hall he opened another door. "Guest room."

Across the hall from that one was another door. It

stood open displaying an office. "I have a larger office, with all the stud records and all down near the main barn. This is more for household accounts and the like."

He passed the next door, heading straight for the one at the end of the hall, but she stopped by it.

"What's in here?"

He turned, paused and slowly came back up to her, opening the door.

"It was the nursery. John-Michael used it until he was older and moved to the room he currently has."

She opened the door and looked in. It was dusty and dark, with closed shades on the windows. The furniture that which a baby would use.

It seemed a sad, neglected room, reflecting the hopes gone wrong from a marriage. Amanda was sorry she had opened the door.

"One more and we're done." Mac pulled the door shut and continued to the end of the hall.

The last door opened to reveal the master bedroom. Again, sliding glass doors opened on to the deck, framing the mountains in a living mural. A large bed dominated the room, rich brown coverlet reaching the floor. A triple dressing-table and tall wardrobe filled one wall, yet were not too much for the room's size. A dressing room and bathroom led off from the back.

Amanda's heart began thudding in her chest. This was Mac's room. Where he slept at night, got dressed each day. She looked around, taking in all the details, storing them in her memory for the future.

She'd be able to envisage him here when she was on tour, when she was away from Timber. Moving further into the room, she looked out the window to learn the view he saw first thing each morning.

The door clicked shut.

Spinning round, Amanda found Mac close to her, disturbingly close.

"It's a nice place," she said huskily, Mesmerized by his gaze.

Without reply he reached out and slowly drew her into his arms, as if giving her time to pull away, should she so desire. Which she didn't.

She went right into his arms as if she belonged there. Her kisses were hot and sweet and as loving as she could make them. She wanted to know this man better. Spend time with him. Have him want to spend time with her. Explore whether the feelings of love had depth or was it only infatuation?

Amanda was aching with desire. She knew there must be more, must be a completion of the longings he had aroused; how to find it?

"Mandy." Mac continued moving his hand gently over her curves, lifting his head a little.

She opened her eyes to meet his gaze. Mac was no longer so disapproving, but looked under a strain.

"What?" she replied, moving beneath his touch.

"I didn't mean for this to happen, you know," he replied, his eyes holding hers.

She licked her lips; it was hard to concentrate on what he was saying; she wanted to lose herself in his touch.

"What?" she repeated.

He gave her a quick kiss. "This. Me and you. Will you marry me, Mandy?"

Twelve

Her eyes flew open in shocked surprise. Stepping back she stared at him. Had she heard him correctly?

"Do you mean it? Marriage?"

He watched her. "Yes, of course I mean it. Do you think I go round asking everyone I meet?"

"No, but I thought you didn't even like me. That you wanted me to move."

"Well, I did at first. I disapprove of your lifestyle, your choice of friends. We fight almost every time we get together, but I still keep thinking of reasons to seek you out, of getting us together again. This last week has been the longest I've ever spent. I felt sick earlier when you said this festival may be the only one you'll go to. You could move on. I've been fighting a losing battle ever since that kiss by the creek."

She gave a soft gurgle of laughter, remembering the pan of water she'd thrown at him. Then her face softened.

A dream come true. The man she loved wanted to marry her.

She paused. She thought he loved her but he hadn't said so in words.

She opened her mouth to ask, but was forestalled.

"Don't answer right away, unless you can say yes. I've been thinking long and hard on it, especially since last week. I can't think when you're looking at me like that," he growled softly in her ear. She took another step back, fascinated by what he had to say.

"We don't know each other very well," she began, "and don't agree on basic issues, like a wife working..." Amanda said, wanting all doubts swept away.

"I know we don't, but I've been thinking a lot this past week or so. Perhaps there's something to a woman working outside the house. The modern conveniences we enjoy don't make keeping a home very challenging. If you feel strongly that you want to work, then I'll gladly share your life with your job."

Now would be the time to tell him what she did, why it'd be more than sharing just a job with someone who left each morning and came home that night. There'd be weeks on the road, quick trips to Nashville, to Los Angeles, to other major cities if they had a concert. She needed to tell him--

He shook his head. "No, let me finish. As to knowing each other, I only have fifty or so years I can set aside to get to know you. Won't that be enough?

"We have a similar feeling for the countryside around here. You're kind to children, witness John-Michael and his guitar lessons. You aren't the usual kind of woman I've met in recent years. I want to spend as much of my time with you as I can."

"Fifty years might be long enough. I'd love to marry

you, Mac." She reached up to kiss him.

"My life was torn apart once by the festival. Maybe this year it'll put it back together."

"I hope so. Oh, Mac, love me." Amanda reached her arms around his neck, giving herself up to his embrace. There was so much to discuss, to clarify--her career, his first marriage. But now, there was only Mac and her and their love.

"Dad?" John-Michael's voice could be heard from a distance. Mac went suddenly still.

"Dad?" John-Michael was closer.

"What would I give for some uninterrupted time." Mac asked, swiftly opening the door. "Phones, aunts, kids. What next?"

"Hi, Dad. Ted and I fixed that stretch of fence." John-Michael stood in the hall while Mac blocked entry into his room.

Amanda's her heart sang!

She was officially engaged to marry John MacKensie. A smile of sheer happiness spread across her face as her spirits soared. Who'd have thought the bus ride to Timber would end so happily? She'd be with him all the time, when she wasn't on tour.

Oh, oh. What would Mac say when she told him what she did for a living? That the job he'd be sharing her with involved weeks when she'd be away from home, traveling, leading a totally different life from the one in Timber.

He knew nothing about her current life.

With his temper, he'd explode when she told him. He thought he knew all that was important--she was a hippie from Colorado.

Okay, so she'd just wait a little longer. Until he was in a good, loving mood again, not now when he was frustrated by another interruption. For the time being, she'd savor this moment. Savor the love she felt for him. Her own, darling, disapproving Mac.

"No." Mac sounded exasperated. Amanda turned to watch him, love evident in her face, in her eyes as she moved to be near him. Mac ran a hand through his hair, still blocking the door.

"No, what?" Amanda asked.

"That's torn it." He turned and John-Michael slowly leaned in the doorway, grinning when he saw Amanda standing in his dad's room.

"Hi, Mandy."

"Hi, yourself, John-Michael."

She tried to maintain her composure in the face of this kid with the knowing grin.

"Come on, Mandy, I'll take you home." Mac reached for her hand, leading her out. As he passed by John-Michael he stopped, looking at his son.

"Mandy's going to marry me," he said, watching the expressions chase across his son's face, from incredulity to disbelief to delight.

"Hey, that's great!"

The boy swept Mandy up in a robust hug. "Wait until I tell the guys."

"I'll be back later." Mac led the way to the truck, throwing Amanda a friendly smile as they climbed in.

She was warmed by his look and smiled back, feeling

187

as if she were floating on air. She still couldn't believe it.

"You coming in?" she asked when they reached the cabin.

"You bet, I am. We were interrupted."

She laughed. "Again."

Climbing out of the truck, she heard her phone ringing. "I'll run and get it. That way they won't have to call back and maybe interrupt anything."

Probably whoever was calling would hang up before she could reach it, but she'd try. Made it, she thought as she snatched it up.

"Mandy? Mandy, this is Dave. Evie fell down a flight of stairs. She's in the hospital and ... oh, Mandy, she's not doing well. Can you come? I need you, cuz, they ... they don't know if Evie will make it. Or the baby. I don't know what I'll do if she dies. Mandy, I need you. Please."

Amanda closed her eyes against the pain in his voice. Her dear cousin--what an awful thing to happen. They were so happy and so looking forward to their baby.

"Of course I'll come right away. The baby?"

"They don't know. They don't know if the baby will live or if," he voice broke a little, "if Evie will either. Mandy, what will I do if Evie dies?"

"I'll be there as soon as I can get there. Are you at home or at the hospital?"

"I'm at the hospital, it's St Paul's. I can't see her yet, she's still in surgery. What will I do without Evie? What will I do if she doesn't make it?"

"She will, she will. Hold on Davie. I'll be there as soon as I can make it. Hang in there."

Amanda put down the receiver, tears swimming in her eyes. She turned. Mac was blocking the door, his face impassive.

"Oh, Mac, I've got to go. I've got to get home. Can you take me ..." Where? She wanted to get to an airport, a plane "d be the fastest way to get to Los Angeles. Even at that it'd take hours.

"Where's the nearest airport? Maybe I can get a flight to L.A. My cousin's has a bad fall. She, she may not make it."

Amanda dashed away the tears, finding herself in Mac's warm arms.

"Easy, girl, we'll get you to an airport. Stockton's only an hour or so away. I'll call for reservations then we'll go. You get what you need while I call."

"Thanks, Mac."

She drew strength from him, gave him a last hug then hurried to throw a few things in her shoulder bag. She still had her things in her L.A. Apartment. Clothes were the last of her worries right now.

"Ready." She ran out to the living room.

Her furniture was in and arranged nicely, totally changing the appearance of the cabin. There was even a sofa, as Mac had once wanted. He didn't even have a chance to comment on it.

"Let's go. I booked you on the 6 pm. flight, it's the last direct one out. We'll make it."

The drive down to Stockton was a total blur to Amanda. She was worried about her cousin, and about Evie. Dave had always been so strong. To have him so

189

distraught was frightening.

She prayed Evie at least would be spared. And the baby. What had happened? From what stairs had she fallen to be so gravely injured? Their apartment building had elevators. Please let Evie be all right, for Dave's sake. Please, she prayed.

"I won't waste time trying to park. I'll drop you off. We're cutting it close, but you'll make it," Mac said as they took the airport exit from Highway 99.

Amanda hadn't realized they were so near. Her mind was whirling, she couldn't concentrate on anything but getting to Evie and Dave.

"Fine, that will be fine." She gathered her things as he pulled up before the airline.

She looked at him. "Thank you, Mac."

He kissed her lightly, his eyes very somber. "Come back, Mandy."

"Of course." She got out and hurried into the airport.

From Stockton to Los Angeles was less than an hour and a half. To Amanda it seemed endless. Her thoughts were in turmoil. Scarcely believing the misfortune that had befallen Dave, she tried to imagine what had happened, how Evie could have fallen, and so seriously. She was scared.

She wished she Mac had come with her.

Mac. How quickly their special moment had vanished.

How different things might be had John-Michael not come home early.

Though she couldn't have reached Los Angeles today had she not heard the news exactly when she did. Wistfully

190

she wished she could have remained in ignorance for just a little longer. She'd had so little time with Mac and their words of love.

A night of inactivity or worry and long-distance concern would have been worse, she supposed. Her heart ached for Dave. How devastated she'd be if anything happened to Mac. And she and he hadn't yet had time together to grow closer, to develop an interdependent loving partnership, to forge a life together.

Hurry, she urged the jetliner, hurry, hurry.

By the time Amanda reached St Paul's Hospital she was calm, her emotions firmly under control. What would be, would be. She needed to be strong for Dave no matter what.

She found her cousin, with Sam and Phil, in the intensive care waiting area. Dave's face lightened when he saw her and he strode across the tiled floor to hug her in a tight embrace.

How's Evie?" she asked immediately.

His reply was shaky. "Holding on. They delivered the baby by C-section. It's a girl. Evie wanted a girl."

"I know and you want what Evie wants."

They moved to join the others.

"Hi, guys."

"Mandy."

"Hi, sugar. Bad scene, isn't it?" Sam gave her a hug.

"I'll say. When will they know more?" she asked.

Sam shrugged, looked at Dave, then replied, "Seems the longer she holds on, the better her chances are. They just don't know."

"What happened?"

Dave told her of Evie's fall down the concrete stairs leading from a friend's second floor apartment. She'd hit her head severely and it was that trauma which was life threatening.

"And the baby? Have you seen her? What's her name?"

Dave shook his head. "She's in guarded condition, whatever that means. Hasn't had a very good birthday."

The hours stretched out as they talked softly, comforted each other and waited for news from the doctors.

It was close to midnight when a weary resident came to tell them to go home. They didn't anticipate any change before morning, if then, but would call instantly if there were any.

The hospital was going on its night shift, usually the quietest time at St Paul's. They'd all be better rested the next day if they got a good night's sleep tonight.

Dave was finally convinced. Amanda went home with him. They'd all be back in the morning.

The days dragged by. Evie's condition stabilized, but she remained in a coma. The baby, in spite of her shaky beginning, was soon thriving. When she was discharged from the hospital at the end of a week, Amanda took charge, calling her Davie's Baby.

Dave refused to name the child, claiming that he'd wait for Evie.

The entire band was back in Los Angeles by this time,

rallying around, taking turns sitting with Dave at Evie's bedside or helping Amanda with the baby.

As the days passed, Amanda gradually assumed some of the managerial roles Dave usually performed.

The second week she was there, she suggested they begin rehearsals for the forthcoming album. She tried the new songs from Bob Clive and immediately decided to include them.

Her two songs from early in the summer were already on the list. She introduced the one she'd just finished. The others approved, both of the song and the sentiments it expressed.

Explanations were shared and congratulations given for her engagement. Now if only Dave approved.

Twice Amanda called Mac, but he sounded distant and reserved the first time. He was out when she called again. She spoke at length to John-Michael, leaving her number and telling him what was going on. And, that it looked like her trip would last longer than she'd thought.

She got Elizabeth Burke's number from John-Michael and called to reassure that they'd be there in plenty of time for the festival, but might not come prior to the day itself.

Amanda didn't want the older woman to become concerned because of Amanda's lengthy absence.

The days were full, the nights dragged. Uncertainties and doubts arose as she lay awake long into the night.

Mac had never out loud said he loved her.

Could he be so obsessed with acquiring the land that he'd resort to marriage?

She didn't want to believe that. He'd dropped that

topic once she had given him the option agreement.

She thought he cared for her, wanted her. She must be important for him to propose marriage. An affair would be less permanent from his viewpoint but he hadn't suggested that.

Then, why not call her? Why the long silence on his part? Maybe he didn't like the telephone, but surely he'd want to make some contact with her.

Maybe if she gave him her address, he'd write. That seemed even less likely. Somehow Amanda didn't see him with a pen in hand. Would he be any more likely to send her an email? Calling would be much easier.

Maybe he regretted his hasty proposal made in a moment of passion. Perhaps he'd had second thoughts.

Amanda didn't know what to think. She only knew she ached all over with loneliness and longing.

As Amanda was bathing Davie's Baby one morning, the phone rang. A jubilant Dave was calling to tell her Evie was conscious, aware, and the doctors gave their prognosis of a full, though slow, recovery.

All the members of the band were overjoyed and relieved with the news. Life again became pleasurable. Activity picked up, preparing the bus for the trip to Timber and the autumn concert tour, testing all the equipment, last-minute rehearsals, Dave joining in at last.

Plans and confirmations of reservations were handled for the autumn tour, everything was falling into place. The schedule set for recording.

The days became more and more hectic as loose ends were wrapped up, as life geared up again for a concert tour of spanning thirty performances.

The idyllic getaway summer was over.

Evie was home. Dave back with the band, the baby named–Annie for her grandmother--and the world was right again.

Amanda tried again and again to talk to Mac, but only talked with John-Michael.

"Tell your father I'll be there Labor Day for the festival. For sure. You're going this year, aren't you?"

"Yes, for the first time. Shall we meet you before you sing?"

"Heavens, yes. We'll be there about ten, I hope. You and your dad get there around then, too. I don't have to do much with the set up. The guys do that part. I can't wait to see you again. To see your dad."

"Are you coming by bus?"

"Yes, my own this time," she said carelessly. "We'll drive straight to the fairground."

"We'll see you about ten, then, Amanda," John-Michael replied.

She had still not talked to John- Michael to see how he knew who she was. There'd be time. When she got to Timber.

"Good. Tell your father ..." There was so much she wanted to say. But not through a third person. "Tell him I said hi."

Thirteen

The next stop would be the fairground in Timber! Amanda and the guys in her band had driven up from Los Angeles in the big black and silver bus, *Amanda* emblazoned on its side. After a night's stop-over in Stockton, the bus was on the last leg of the journey to Timber. They'd arrive right on time for setting up for the performance at the festival. Sam was at the wheel, making the curvy mountain hills seem like easy driving as he babied the bus around bends, coaxed it up the hills, coasted down.

Amanda was impatient to reach their destination. She couldn't wait to see Mac. They still had lots to discuss, decisions and plans to make. All that notwithstanding, she was just plain dying to see him again, to be with him.

While super glad she'd been able to help her cousin, she still felt a little short-changed for her own summer, her own engagement, the only one she'd have.

She planned to stay married to one man for life, believing in the old until-death-do-us-part words. She wasn't a young girl, infatuated by love's first breath, but a mature woman, sure in herself, confident in the love she felt for Mac MacKensie.

Still, it'd have been nice to have had a normal engagement. She didn't even know when he wanted to get married! There had been no long walks together, just the two of them; no intimate dinners; no time to really get to know each other. She smiled, remembering he had said he only had fifty years left. Would it be enough? She doubted it.

She'd called and told her parents. They wanted to meet him, of course, but couldn't leave the ranch at this time. She promised they'd find time to visit Colorado before Christmas.

Hurry, she urged the bus, just as she had once urged a big jet. This time it was for herself. Hurry. Hurry.

As they drew near, drew close to the river called Mokelumne, Amanda sat on the edge of her seat. It was with growing pleasure she recognized landmarks now. Soon, very soon, they'd be there.

Yes, here was the bridge. Soon they'd turn left, take that road to the festival grounds. She was sure of the directions, Elizabeth had been specific. There, that's where it was. Hurry.

Sam pulled the big bus into the gravel parking area by the festival grounds, swinging wide around the cars already parked, slowing for the pedestrians in the lot.

Amanda was surprised at the number of people there, already working getting things ready. Already visiting with friends and neighbors.

The concession stands were being erected. Tables and tents for the arts and crafts section were going up. In the distance, volley-ball nets were being strung; iron stakes pounded in for horseshoes.

Sam skillfully maneuvered the big bus close to the portable stage erected on the grass at the far end of the field, near the parking lot. As the bus lumbered along, crunching gravel, spurting dust from beneath its wheels, heads turned, speculation ran riot.

Several people wandered near the vehicle, then a few more. When Sam finally stopped and opened the door, one bold teenager approached.

"Is this bus for Amanda, the country singer?"

"Sure is, miss," he answered cheerfully, giving her a big grin as he climbed out.

"Riverboat Gambler Amanda?" called another.

Sam smiled and nodded.

"Oh, wow!"

The word began to spread.

Dave, Joe and the others quickly joined Sam and fell into their routine, to set up as they did for all the shows, unloading equipment, putting it in place on the stage. Stringing electric cable, connectors. Testing the instruments, the amplifiers. More and more people were drawn to watch, some to stake out good seats. Others to speculate with friends as they kept a watchful eye on the activities.

Amanda hung back, remained in the bus. She wasn't usually a part of this. Her job came later, during the show. For now she was free to stay in the bus, her eyes searching the parking lot for a beat-up old gray pick-up truck. She fairly seethed with impatience. Where was he?

Her hair was clean, shiny and newly trimmed. It waved

and curled around her face, framing it softly, catching highlights in the sun. She wore a silver outfit, fringed and embroidered, remembering he'd said the color would suit her. Her make-up was on, she was ready.

Where was Mac? It was after ten. Where was he?

She saw the fancy truck turning into the parking lot, driving slowly towards the bus. Her heart lodged in her throat. Mac. She scrambled from the bus eager to see him. She'd missed him so much!

"Amanda, can I have your autograph?" One girl, leaning against the bus, thrust a paper and pencil in her face. "I'm so excited to meet you. I can't wait to hear you sing. I didn't know you were the main attraction. Boy, am I glad I came to the festival this year."

"Can I have your autograph, too?" another asked.

"Me, too?" still another clamored.

There were a dozen or more young people surrounding her, exclaiming their happiness at her being at the festival, smiling shyly at the famous star in their midst. Eager to gain her attention, to obtain the personal favor of an autograph.

And impeding her progress.

Smiling, Amanda signed each request, impatience seething within her, outwardly serene and at ease with the group, answering questions, writing what was asked of her. She was where she was in the industry today because of her fans. She'd be gracious and patient and smiling and...

There, the last one signed. With a smile all round, she moved eagerly to the pick-up.

A feeling of deja vu. Mac leaning against the side, arms crossed, face frowning.

Amanda's heart sank. She didn't blame him for being angry, there was a lot she'd never told him. What a way for him to find it out, too, just arrive and be slapped in the face with the big bus, the crowds, all the things he'd never suspected about her.

She wished more than ever that she'd told him of her career and why she was spending the summer incognito. Their time had been cut too short.

He hated deceit. He'd been very clear about his view point that the day of the picnic in the big clearing. She'd have to give a good reason of why she hadn't told him initially who she was, what she did.

But later.

Now she was so very glad to see him; wasn't he glad to see her?

"Hi, Mac." She stopped close to him, tilting her head back to smile so happily up at him, shocked at the glittering green eyes, the lines of disapproval.

"The famous Amanda deigned to visit the mountain yokels one more time. A triumphant return, I might add."

"I can explain ..." she began. Oh, oh, it looks like explanations must come now, not later.

"Save your lies Amanda. I've been fooled before and God help me it looks as if I have been again."

"No."

Mac stood up, towering above her anger radiating from every inch of him.

"What a fun summer you must have had--have a fling with some gullible local, then high-tail it back to Los Angeles and your lover there when things start turning serious here. Well, serious is off, now. You've had your fun and I've had mine. I should have taken more when I had the chance, but we're even now, and quits!"

"Mac, please listen."

Amanda was scared. She put a tentative hand on his arm. Had she ruined everything by her desire for secrecy, by her wish to be just plain Mandy Smith for a summer? He had to listen. Then he'd understand. He had to!

He glanced at her hand in disgust, shaking it off.

"Next time, pretend a little more, Amanda. At least tell the guy once that you love him, even though it'll be a lie, too."

"I do love you. It's not a lie. Listen to me."

She was close to tears; he couldn't be so implacable that he wouldn't even listen to her.

"I've heard it all before, Mandy, from Liza," he ground out, turned and stalked away, back rigid with disapproval.

Amanda started to follow, but was again impeded then blocked by more fans clamoring for autographs. As her identity spread, more and more of Timber's residents came over, some for pictures and one or two that she knew to speak to her.

The girl who had been so friendly in the drugstore came over. "Fancy you being so famous. I don't think we'll call it Cora's house much longer."

Amanda laughed with her, though her eyes scanned the crowds, trying to locate Mac.

Her heart was breaking. How could she have been so stupid not to find a moment to tell him?

Martin Roberts came up to her reminiscing about the

day she bought Cora's house. Pam Haversham joined them, then Elizabeth Burke and lastly, John- Michael. Elizabeth gave her a hug.

"My dear, John-Michael tells me you're quite famous, that it's quite a feather in our cap to have you for our festival. I'm so pleased, but I'm sorry I didn't realize it before. We are indebted to you for joining us today."

"I'm glad to do it, Elizabeth. I still plan to make Timber my home. I want to contribute to my home town's events, too. If it's something people like, good."

John-Michael gave her a quick hug much to the amazement of the onlookers.

"Glad to see you, Mom," he teased.

Amanda threw him an anguished look. "I'm not sure it's still on. Your dad's so mad at me."

"Mac? Nonsense. He'll be delighted to find out who you are and that the festival has such outstanding talent today. He'll like it when he sees all we've done," Elizabeth said firmly. "I'm so glad he came this year."

Amanda smiled, nodding.

"John-Michael, why did you call her Mom?" Pam Haversham asked, picking up on his words.

He looked questioningly at Amanda, then grinned at Pam. "I guess they're announcing it today. Dad's asked her to marry him." John-Michael grinned proudly.

Elizabeth stared at them, first one, then the other, mouth open. Finally summoning her wits she said, "I never thought I'd see the day. Welcome to the family, child. Good gracious!" She gave Amanda a tight hug.

"Well, I'm surprised," Pam added. "Best wishes and all

that!" She hugged Amanda as well.

"Thanks, Pam, I..."

"Time for a last minute check, Mandy," Dave called from the bus.

Excusing herself with a promise to join them all after the show, she moved to the bus.

"Where's the happy groom?" Dave asked, scanning the crowds much as Amanda had done moments earlier. His beard was trimmed for the show, his cowboy outfit ornate with silver and embroidery.

"Flaming angry with me," she replied, climbing into the bus.

Briefly, while she refreshed her make-up, she explained. While her cousin disliked the thought of her living so far away from the action, he understood her desire to marry the one man she thought would bring her as much happiness as his Evie brought him.

"I'll talk to him, if you like," Dave offered when she had finished.

"I can't use a go-between all my life. Thanks anyway. I'll just hunt him up after the show and make him listen to me. I have some rights in this, too, you know," she said spiritedly.

"Show time." Joe popped his head in.

Taking a deep breath, Amanda gave a dazzling smile. "I'm ready."

The day was warm, the sun shone in a cloudless sky, a gentle breeze kept the air temperate. There were people milling around, some playing the games at the far end of the field. Many were still eating, enjoying the festive atmosphere, enjoying the camaraderie of their friends and neighbors in this, the last big community event before the inclement weather forced people to stay indoors.

The majority of the town, however, was seated on the benches and chairs set up for the entertainment event or sprawled on blankets spread for the best view of the stage.

Amanda and Dave walked together to the steps at the rear of the portable stage. The disjointed twang of guitars being timed, of amplifiers being adjusted, could be heard over the noise of the crowd.

Amanda paused, feeling the surge of adrenaline that preceded performances. She loved it. The excitement, the challenge of bringing pleasure and entertainment to hundreds of people. All through the gift of music that had been given to her.

She knew she was fortunate in her chosen field. A lot of luck went into their achieving stardom and in such a relatively short time--less than ten years. Still, they'd all worked hard to be where they were, Dave, Sam, Joe, Marc, and Phil. They were a team and she never wanted to give it up, not completely.

If she married Mac, no, she lifted her chin, when she married Mac, she'd curtail some of the traveling, but not all. She loved it too much to quit.

He'd have to take this part of her as well as the rest of her. This career contributed to making her the person she was today, the one he'd asked to marry him.

She heard the opening music, mounted the stairs and burst out into view to the thunderous applause of the citizens of Timber. Taking the microphone from Dave with a bright smile, she launched immediately into the first song, "Riverboat gambler, you take too many chances."

The applause rose as the audience expressed their approval, drowning out the first few lines, then died away as everyone settled back to enjoy familiar songs performed by a top professional.

Amanda did her best for her new town, her band backing her to the limit. As she sang, joyfully, with great enthusiasm, she let her eyes browse through the crowd, recognizing people here and there; a committee member she met at Elizabeth's; the old man from the bus depot; John-Michael. With a small shock she saw Mac seated beside his son, his aunt on his other side.

His hat was pulled low, shading his features. Her eyes passed on. Sally Sutherland and her father were on the far side of Elizabeth; Pam and Ron Haversham back towards the rear of the crowd.

When she finished her first song she moved right into Heartbroken Dreamer.--another popular song. And then another. And another.

When the series ended, the band became quiet. Amanda, smiling brightly, waited for the applause to die down, then spoke to the crowd.

"Happy Labor Day."

She smiled again as the people clapped, whistled, yelled back. It was an exuberant group. Easy to please, warm and friendly.

"Thank you for your warm welcome. We're glad to be here."

Again she had to pause, happiness and goodwill welling

up inside her at the enthusiastic reception.

"I'd like to introduce everyone up here. As a lot of you already know, we're a family group. Didn't plan on it, it just happened. We all grew up together in a little town outside Durango, in Colorado. Played together, ventured forth together. And, here we are. On the drums, cousin Sam Perkins, on Mama's side, you know. Bass guitar, Phil Perkins, Sam's brother. Rhythm guitar, Joe Williams, Mama's side again. Electric piano, Marc Johnson. Mama's part of a large family."

The crowd, applauding after each introduction, roared with laughter.

"My main man, manager, promoter, dearest friend and cousin, on Daddy's side, Dave Smith."

Amanda waited for silence before continuing.

"As some of you know, I moved to Timber a few months ago, bought Cora Rosenfeld's old place. I figure in fifty years or so you will call it Mandy's old place, or old Mandy's place, by then ... Timber's a grand place to live..."

The crowd wouldn't let her continue, they showed their approval in a thunderous round of applause.

"I've written a few songs since I've been here. I want to share them with you. If they bomb out, maybe as neighbors, you'll let me down easy."

She nodded to Dave and, when the clapping diminished, the music started.

"Bluebells on the hill, nodding in the hot Sierra sun..." She sang the song she'd first written, in the early days of her life in Timber, to an enthusiastic response.

She followed it with the second one she wrote. Moving

into a duet with Dave, a slow ballad, then song after song made famous over the last five years. All were recognized, liked, popular. The program ran far, far longer than Elizabeth's estimated hour, but no one seemed anxious for it to end.

Finally she dropped the microphone beside her legs, turning to Dave for a quick moment, then back to then audience.

"Two more and we'll call it quits."

Groans and protests arose from the townsfolk. She raised a hand.

"One of them is the most recent one I wrote here."

She licked her lips nervously, again looked at Dave, grinning at her.

"Remember," she said for him alone, "when this one is done, go right into Sing the Mountain Down. Don't pause at all."

"They'll love it," he encouraged.

She took a breath, waiting for the music's cue.

Her strong, clear alto rose over the crowd, filling every corner of the field with the sweet harmony, the words sung simply, clearly and from her heart.

"She didn't need the mike," one listener said afterward.

"Beautiful, strong voice, lovely song," said another.

"Did you see his face?" asked a third. "I watched him, you know, I saw it."

Amanda's voice carried conviction as her voice swelled for the chorus, her eyes only for Mac now,

"... I love a rancher ... I love a rancher ..."

Mac stared back at her, too far away for Amanda to see

him clearly, to see how he was taking her song. She noticed John-Michael looked at his dad, with a grin as big as his face, but Mac steadfastly stared at Amanda.

And glory be, glory be, ... the rancher loves me..."

People turned to look at Mac, neighbor nudging neighbor as the word spread. Grins appeared on faces, attention split between the singer and Mac MacKensie.

"Look at his eyes." A neighbor nudged a friend.

"The song's about Mac MacKensie."

"The song's right, too, he looks as if he adores her," the friend replied.

Again and again the chorus rang out, filling the festival ground of Timber, California, filling the people's minds and hearts with delight.

"... I love a rancher ... and glory be, the rancher loves me ..."

The audience went wild. Stood as they clapped and whistled and cheered. On and on the thunderous ovation continued. Amanda blinked her eyes, trying to clear them of the tears that blurred her vision, smiling tremulously at the people.

She turned to Dave, with a questioning look; why no lead into the next song? He just smiled and shrugged. No point, who'd hear with the noise the audience was making?

Amanda turned back to the crowd. She could no longer see Mac, nor others she knew, just a sea of happy, applauding fans. She bowed again and again, happy they liked her song.

How had Mac liked it? That was the real question.

As soon as the tumult died a little, Dave started up the

music. Sing the Mountain Down had hit the top of the charts, was still very popular and soon she was well into it. Into it and finished. At last, the show was over.

Again and again she bowed her thanks for their applause, motioning to the band, to Dave. Smiling, waving. Finally, for the last time.

Then she turned and walked quickly back to the rear of the stage, stumbled down the steps, right into Mac's arms.

"I was an idiot," he murmured, gathering her in and lowering his head.

The touch of his mouth drove all conscious thought from Amanda's head. She clasped him tightly and returned his kisses, hungry for them. Longing and desire rose. Wishing the moment could go on and on, only the two of them, together again at last. His mouth warm and exciting, his hands molding her against him.

"Was that a proposal up there?" he asked, when he at last raised his head.

"Please, I'm an engaged lady, I don't make proposals."

She smiled up at him, love shining from her eyes, oblivious to all going on around them.

"It was quite a song. You have a beautiful way with words, sweetheart."

"Like, I love you?"

Um, just like that." He lowered his head again to her waiting lips.

"Excuse us, but you're blocking the way." Dave stood on the bottom step, Sam and Joe close behind.

"Oh, sorry. Dave, Sam, Joe, this is Mac!" Amanda turned around, smiling in her happiness, linking her arm in his and introducing him.

"We've sort of met," Dave said, hesitantly offering a hand.

"Yes." Mac took it. "But with a misconception; I thought you were her biker lover."

Amanda giggled. That was something else to be cleared up. She'd forgotten Mac was still in the dark about a lot of things.

"Biker!" Dave sputtered, outrage evident in his face. Sam kindly bumped him along before he could explode.

"Glad to meet the rancher. How did you like her song?"

Joe also shook his hand, as did Phil and Marc, now joining them.

"I liked the song. I expect most of the town liked it." he said dryly. "I wasn't expecting anything like it. I've never had a song written to me before." He turned and glanced warmly at Amanda's upturned face. "I liked it very much," he repeated.

"We thought it was good, too."

Mac turned back to the band. "I reckon I'll be seeing a lot of you all, if I throw my lot in with her," Mac said, drawing her close.

"Right on," Dave said, still annoyed at being thought a biker. "But from what Mandy has lined up, not until October."

One or two other people were coming around the stage, more behind them.

"I'll look forward to it," Mac said hastily, his eye on the group approaching.

He turned them toward the parking lot.

"I have a few things I want cleared up, are you finished? Can we leave?"

"Yes, let's go. See you later," she called over her shoulder. "Enjoy the picnic."

In only moments, they were pulling out of the parking lot, leaving the crowds behind, just the two of them heading for the ranch.

"I'm sorry you found out the way you did," Amanda began diffidently. "I don't blame you a bit for being so angry. I wanted to tell you earlier in the summer, but never found the right time. Then the rest happened so fast, your proposal, John-Michael's interruption, then the news about Evie."

"How is she, by the way," Mac interrupted.

"Oh, she's coming along fine. Complete recovery expected. She's Dave's wife, you know. I'm very fond of her."

"No, I didn't know Dave was married. In fact, I know very little about you other than you're headstrong and stubborn and fill my days with joy," Mac replied.

A lump caught in her throat at the unexpected compliment.

"Oh, Mac, I've missed you so much."

"I've missed you, too. I thought the time would never pass. Each night seemed five years long. Then to drive in this morning and see that bus." He drew in a ragged breath. "John-Michael told me who you really were. He knew, but hadn't said anything."

"I should have told you before, but with one thing and

another, I just didn't. We could have talked over the weeks, but you never returned any of my calls. I'm sorry you found out that way this morning."

"I didn't want an impersonal call on the hone. And when you didn't come home after a week or two, I began to believe it was because you didn't want to."

"I had to help with Evie. I wanted to write, then thought I should tell you personally about things. Don't be mad. I missed you so much," she said, reaching out to touch him

"Tell me about you," he said, reaching out to hold her hand.

So Amanda did, all about the incognito summer, about Dave and Evie and baby Annie.

"And so I wrote the song. I could never seem to come out and tell you," she finished.

He pulled into the driveway and stopped, turning to her.

"But, Mandy love, I especially want you to say whatever you like to me. For you to feel safe and secure in our life together, to be at ease always with me. I made mistakes in my first marriage. I don't plan to repeat them this go round. If I live to be a hundred-and-three, I want you there with me, singing your songs, panning for gold, whatever it is you want."

"I want to be with you," she said softy. "I love you, Mac."

"I love you, sweetheart."

He took her in his arms, kissing her deeply as a man long deprived, his mouth warm and exciting, evoking the responses Amanda remembered all so well. Eagerly she returned his kiss, her mouth a soft inviting sweetness to him. Slowly she trailed fingers down the strong column of his neck, slipping beneath the collar of his shirt. His skin was warm and taut.

He left her mouth to trail kisses along her neck, to her cheeks.

"What about Sally Sutherland?" she asked abruptly.

Mac drew back just a little. "Sally? What about Sally?"

He was totally at a loss.

"Well, she was very possessive at your aunt's dinner party and then sat near you today and all," Amanda vaguely trailed off. "I thought perhaps you had something."

"I fell in love with a hot-tempered brat the day I kissed her and she doused me with icy water. I've never loved Sally, nor given her two thoughts since falling in love with you."

"That's when?" She laughed. "But I had no idea!"

"Well, no," he replied rather sheepishly. "I, er, had to break down my own reservations first. But that's why I arranged for the option. I thought I could tie up the land for the future and be able to stop trying to get you to leave. That was the last thing I wanted by that time."

"And I never knew. I thought I might give you the land for a wedding present."

"Thanks for the thought, but I don't seem to have the same urgency for it now. I'd rather have you."

"Oh, well, it will be in the family. You were a long time in overcoming your own reservations."

He pulled her against him again. "Yes, but once gone,

there was only you. Here I thought I was going to have to reform a hippie wife and find instead a leading star in my life."

"You don't mind too much, do you? she asked anxiously. "I am planning to settle down. My engagements won't be too extensive."

"As long as you always come back to me, I can spare you to the rest of the world a few times a year, I guess."

"I love you John MacKensie."

"And I love you, Mandy Smith."

His mouth was warm and exciting and she arched against him, wondering if they'd ever be close enough to satisfy, to find fulfillment of the promise of his touch.

Releasing her at long last, he sat back, started the truck, reversing out to the highway.

"Are we going back to the picnic?" Amanda asked in surprise.

"No, Nevada. We can get there in only a couple of hours."

"Nevada, whatever for?"

She had thought they'd go to her cabin or his home. Be alone for a while, catch up on things.

"Two reasons, one, they have twenty-four-hour marriage chapels with no waiting, and two, a motel where the phone won't ring, nor kids interrupt, nor aunts drop by. Dave said you don't have commitments until October. We can get started on a honeymoon at least."

Amanda gave a gurgle of laughter. "Oh, Mac, I'd love to. But what about the band? Your aunt? John-Michael?"

"We'll tell them when we get back," he said.

She smiled and reached out to touch him. "I'll always remember this. And don't get me wrong, I want to marry you. But my mama's skin me alive if she wasn't at my wedding. My cousins would never get over it. And you need your son there. Really."

The truck slowed, and he eased to the side of the road. Traffic was non-existent. He looked at her.

"I want you so much."

She undid her seat belt and moved across the seat to be as close to him as she could get. "I want you, too. Today, tomorrow, forever. We have family who will rejoice in our happiness. We can't deprive them of sharing in our joy."

He kissed her and then brushed his fingers against her cheek. "When you're right, you're right. So how soon can we get everyone together?"

Amanda laughed. "Just as soon as we can. Let's go tell them all."

Mac turned the truck around.

She sat back to enjoy the ride, to enjoy whatever life brought from this day forward.

"... Glory be, glory be, the rancher loves me."

If you enjoyed this book, you will enjoy the next book in the *Cowboy Hero* series, **Cowboy's Bride**.

More Books by Barbara McMahon

Cowboy Hero
The Cowboy Next Door
Cowboy's Bride
One Stubborn Cowboy
Crazy About a Cowboy
Never Doubt a Cowboy
Cowboy Marshal
Summer Cowboy
Second Chance Cowboy
Movie Star Cowboy

Sweet Reunion Romance Collection
Unexpected Reunion
Unpredictable Reunion
Unanticipated Reunion

The Harts of Texas
Rebel Heart
Tangled Hearts
Reckless Heart

Ultimate Billionaires
The Cynical Sheikh
Falling for the Sheikh
A Sheikh of Her Own
The Unforgettable Sheikh

Rocky Point
Rocky Point Legacy
Rocky Point Reunion
Rocky Point Promise
Rocky Point Hero
Rocky Point Inn
Rocky Point Dawn

The Talmadge Sisters
Letters to Caroline
Michelle's Marriage Deal
Trusting Abby

Tropical Escapes
Island Rendezvous
Come into the Sun
Island Paradise

Sweet Romance Stand-alone Collection
Because of You
Cowboy Charade
I'll Take Forever
Jared's Promise
Mail Order Bride
Not Really Married
Sweet Meant To Be
The Cowboy Comes Home
The Paper Marriage
Trusting Jake
The Banished Bride

A Sweet Clean Christmas Romance Collection
The Christmas Cop
The Cowboy's Special Christmas
A Soldier's Christmas
A Teaspoon of Mistletoe
The Christmas Locket
A Key West Christmas
The Christmas Locket

Made in the USA
Middletown, DE
17 February 2022

61402840R00126